Orin Fowler

History of Fall River

with notices of Freetown and Tiverton

Orin Fowler

History of Fall River
with notices of Freetown and Tiverton

ISBN/EAN: 9783337302665

Printed in Europe, USA, Canada, Australia, Japan

Cover: Foto ©Andreas Hilbeck / pixelio.de

More available books at **www.hansebooks.com**

HISTORY

—— OF ——

FALL RIVER,

WITH NOTICES OF

FREETOWN AND TIVERTON,

AS PUBLISHED IN 1841,

BY REV. ORIN FOWLER, A. M.,

TOGETHER WITH A SKETCH OF THE LIFE OF REV. ORIN FOWLER:
AN EPITOME OF THE MASSACHUSETTS AND RHODE ISLAND
BOUNDARY QUESTION; AN ACCOUNT OF THE GREAT
FIRE OF 1843; AND ECCLESIASTICAL, MANUFAC-
TURING, AND OTHER STATISTICS.

FALL RIVER:

ALMY & MILNE, PRINTERS, DAILY NEWS STEAM PRESS.
....
1862.

ORIN FOWLER.

*Orin Fowler, the eldest son and sixth child of Captain Amos and Rebecca (Dewey) Fowler, was born at Lebanon, Conn., July 29, 1791. His early years were spent in laboring upon his father's farm, though he was engaged for two winters—when he was sixteen and seventeen years old—in teaching a school.

He fitted for college under the instruction of his pastor, the Rev. Mr. Ripley, and entered Williams College in the autumn of 1811. At the end of the first term he took his dismission, and after studying again for a while under Mr. Ripley, and also for one term at the Academy at Colchester, he entered the Sophomore class in Yale College in October, 1812. Here he maintained an excellent standing as a scholar, being distinguished in the more solid, rather than in the more graceful branches. A few months previous to his graduation, he accepted the Preceptorship of the Academy at Fairfield, Conn., and held the place—discharging its duties with great fidelity and acceptance—until the autumn of 1816, when he resigned it, that he might devote himself more exclusively to theological studies,—Dr. Humphrey, then minister of Fairfield, afterwards President of Amherst College, taking the direction of them.

He was licensed to preach on the 14th of October, 1817, by the Association of the Western District of Fairfield County. Having preached occasionally in different places, chiefly in Fairfield County, but without any reference to settlement, he decided in March, 1818, to go on a mission to the Western country. He was ordained with a view to this, at Farmington, at a meeting of the North Association of Hartford County, on the 3d of June following, and the same

---

*From "Annals of the American Pulpit," by William B. Sprague, D. D.

day rode twenty-one miles toward his field of missionary labor. Having spent about one year laboring in Ohio, Kentucky and Indiana, and perhaps some other of the Southwestern States, he returned to New England, by way of Virginia, in the summer of 1819.

Having preached with acceptance at several different places, he accepted an invitation to supply the pulpit at Plainfield, Conn., in the winter of 1819–20, and shortly after received a call to become the pastor of the church. In due time he signified his acceptance of it, and was installed on the 1st of March, 1820.

Mr. Fowler remained the pastor of the church at Plainfield for nearly eleven years, when, owing to some peculiar circumstances existing in the parish, it was thought expedient that he should be dismissed from his pastoral charge ; and this accordingly took place on the 27th of January, 1831. The council, in dissolving the pastoral relation, rendered an unqualified testimony to his Christian and ministerial character.

Almost immediately after leaving Plainfield, his services were required by the church at Fall River, and he was installed there on the 7th of July of the same year, the installation sermon being preached by the Rev. Dr. McEwen, of New London.

In the year 1841, Mr. Fowler delivered three discourses, containing an historical sketch of Fall River from 1620 to that time. In this sketch he referred to the boundary line between Massachusetts and Rhode Island, that had then been in dispute for about a century. Not long after, at a meeting of the citizens of Fall River on the subject of the boundary, Mr. Fowler, without his consent or even knowledge, was placed upon a committee to defend the interests of the town before Commissioners appointed by the two States. This service he promptly and ably performed ; but the Commissioners came to a decision in which the people of Fall River were little disposed to acquiesce, and they resolved upon an effort to prevent the establishment by the Massachusetts Legislature of the line fixed upon by the Commissioners. Mr. Fowler now published a series of papers in the Boston *Atlas*, designed to present before the public mind the historical facts sustaining the claims of Massachusetts ; but even his most intimate friends did not know that he was the author of them. When the authorship was ascertained, there was a general voice in favor of his being chosen to the Senate of the Commonwealth at the next session of the Legislature. He was accordingly elected in the autumn of 1847, and the Senate, chiefly, it is said, through his influence, rejected the report of the Commissioners by a unanimous vote. Such was the estimation in which he came now to be held as a legislator, that in the autumn of 1848, before his Senatorial term had expired, the people of his district elected him to the thirty-first Congress. Here his influence was extensively and benignly felt, and his advocacy of the cheap postage bill, particularly, is said to have been highly effective.

Mr. Fowler, during the time that he was a member of the Massachusetts Senate, supplied his own pulpit, either in person or by proxy, and continued to perform his pastoral duties until the last of November, 1849, when he left Fall River to take his seat in Congress. Agreeably to a previous understanding, he was dismissed from his pastoral charge by the same council that installed his successor, in the spring of 1850.

During his connection with Congress, he often supplied the pulpits in Washington and the vicinity, and preached for the last time in the autumn of 1851. On the night of the 27th of August, 1852, he had a slight attack of illness, but the next day was able to be in his seat in Congress as usual. A day or two after, the attack was repeated, but relief was again obtained after a few hours. It was soon found, however, that his disease, so far from being dislodged from his system, was taking on an alarming form, and that his system was rapidly sinking under it. After he became convinced that his recovery was hopeless, he requested to be left alone with his wife, when he offered a comprehensive and affecting prayer, without wandering or repetition—mentioning especially both the churches of which he had been pastor. After this he began to speak of his spiritual state, and said:—"I have tried to live in peace with God and man." But the difficulty of respiration did not allow him to proceed. He languished until the 3d of September, and then gently fell into his last slumber.

His remains were taken for burial to Fall River, and were received by his former charge, as well as his fellow citizens generally, with every testimony of consideration and respect. His funeral sermon was preached by his successor, the Rev. Mr. Relyea.

Mr. Fowler was married October 16th, 1821, to Amaryllis, fourth daughter of John How Payson, of Pomfret, Conn. They had ~~no~~ two children.

Besides various speeches in Congress, and contributions to periodicals, newspapers, &c., Mr. Fowler published a sermon preached at the ordination of Israel G. Rose, at Canterbury, in 1825 ; a Disquisition on the Evils attending the use of Tobacco, 1833 ; Lectures on the Mode and Subjects of Baptism, 1835 ; History of Fall River, 1841 ; Papers on the Boundary, 1847.

NOTICE.

In the delivery of the following discourses, those portions of them not suited to the services of the Sabbath, were omitted; and some matter suited to the day and the occasion, was delivered, which is not printed. The numerous facts recorded in this Sketch, have been collected, and their accuracy has been tested, by unwearied labor and research. It is believed they may be relied upon as substantially correct.

The author takes pleasure in acknowledging his obligations to the many friends who have assisted his enquiries; and he will only add, that if these discourses shall aid, in the humblest manner, in saving from oblivion the early history of FALL RIVER, and in promoting her future prosperity, he will be amply rewarded.

HISTORICAL SKETCH.

PSALMS XLIV. 1, 2, 3.

We have heard with our ears, O God, our fathers have told us, what work thou
didst in their days, in the times of old. How thou didst drive out the heathen
with thy hand, and plantedst them; how thou didst afflict the people, and cast
them out. For they got not the land in possession by their own sword, neither
did their own arm save them; but thy right hand, and thine arm, and the light
of thy countenance, because thou hadst a favor unto them.

How changed the scene around us this morning, from what our
ancestors beheld, when, one hundred and sixty years ago, they came
and fixed here the place of their habitation, and began the settlement
of this town! The little river that rolls its rapid waters through
our village, imparts its name to our town, and puts in motion a
mass of machinery sufficient to give business and bread to half of
our population; the waters of the beautiful Bay that spreads out her
bosom before us; the hills and the valleys around us; the great river
upon our right, and the rocky mount in our front; these all remain
substantially as they were, while the wolf, the wild cat, the timid
deer, and the untutored savage, claimed this as their ancient and
rightful dominion. But all else, how changed! The thick, dark forests have disappeared; the wild beasts that roamed these forests, are
gone; and the Indians that inhabited these hills and valleys, and here
kindled their council fires, and shouted the war song, have passed
away like the leaves of their native woods. Where then was a
" waste, howling wilderness," we behold cultivated fields and smiling
gardens; instead of savage tribes, we behold communities of civilized
men; instead of the murky Indian hut, we behold comfortable houses,
and large factories, and splendid public edifices; instead of the Indian

canoe, silently darting along our bay in pursuit of the beaver or black
fish, we behold the elegant steamboat and the stately ship proudly
floating on its bosom, laden with the products of other climes; instead of the war-whoop, and the cry of savage cruelty, we hear, all
around the voice of peace and comfort, and listen to the song of
thanksgiving and praise, rising from thousands of grateful hearts to
the throne of the living God.   We are not come together, as were
our fathers, in fear and want, and gloomy bodings, to offer our worship under the spreading trees of the forest, beneath an inclement
sky.   We are assembled in the enjoyment of plenty, and bright vis-
ions of the future; in the temple dedicated to one God, Father, Son
and Holy Ghost; surrounded with everything that makes society
sweet and life happy.

The first twenty-five years of the existence of this Church, is now
completed, and we, as an organized congregation, have reached a
period in our own history, when it seems proper, to review the past,
and thank God, and gird up our loins for the future.

"We have heard with our ears, O God, our fathers have told us,
what work thou didst in their days, in the times of old.   How thou
didst drive out the heathen with thy hand, and plantedst them; how
thou didst afflict the people, and cast them out.   For they got not
the land in possession by their own sword, neither did their own arm
save them; but thy right hand and thine arm, and the light of thy
countenance, because thou hadst a favor to them."   If this passage
had been designed by the sacred writer, to apply to the early settlement of Plymouth Colony, it could not have been more appropriate;
and were our fathers here to write their own memorial, it would certainly begin and end with such sentiments as are breathed in the text
—they would write "Not unto us, O Lord; not unto us, but to thy
name give glory."   While then we sketch the early history of this
place, let us keep our eye steadily fixed upon the hand of God, scarcely
less visible in the first settlement and subsequent prosperity of New
England, than it had been, in planting his ancient covenant people
in the land of Canaan.

It was my original design to present a succinct history of this
Church and Society only.   But as I proceeded in the execution of
my purpose, I was persuaded that a more extended narration might
be profitable, especially to the young: I shall therefore attempt a
brief sketch of the earlier as well as the later history of our village,

including the towns of Fall River and Tiverton, together with Freetown and the neighboring region, so far as is necessary to elucidate the history of our own place.

The order I propose to pursue is, to sketch

I. The Aboriginal History:

II. The Civil History, and

III. The Ecclesiastical History of this place ; and particularly of this church. I begin

I. With the Aboriginal History of this place and vicinity.

The landing of the Pilgrims at Plymouth, took place December 22d, 1620. At that time the Indian name of the country lying between Providence river and Taunton river, was Pokanoket. Indeed the whole country eastward of Seekonk and Providence rivers, comprising what now constitutes Bristol, Plymouth, Barnstable, Dukes and Nantucket counties, was inhabited by tribes known by the general name of Pokanokets, sometimes written Pawkunnaukutts. The territory comprising Bristol, Warren and Barrington, R. I., and a part of Rehoboth, Mass., was inhabited by the tribe called Wampanoags.*

The chief seat of this tribe was at Mount Hope†, called by the Indians Mont-haup, or Mon-top; the more ancient name of the Mount was Pokanoket, or Pawkunnaukutt, a name given by the Narragansetts. Pokanoket signifies "the wood or land on the other side of the water," the appropriateness of which will be seen when it is recollected that the Narragansetts lived on the west side of the waters of the Narragansett Bay. Massasoit was the name of the chief Sachem of the Wampanoags.‡ He was regarded as the chief Sachem of the different petty tribes occupying the whole, or nearly the whole of these five counties, together with Bristol county, Rhode Island, and his authority was recognized by other tribes living farther North. Massasoit kindly welcomed our fathers to these shores, and always lived on terms of sincere friendship with them. He was

---

*This tribe was sometimes called Pokanokets.

†Mount-Hope is about two miles east of Bristol, and within that ancient town. It is an eminence, steep on all sides, and terminating in a large rock, which, at a distance, has the appearance of a large dome of an amphitheatre. From many points on the eastern shore of Mount-Hope Bay, particularly at the village of Fall River, (four or five miles distant,) the Mount forms a beautiful acclivity in the landscape, somewhat resembling a remote view of the State House in Boston.

‡It was the Indian custom frequently to change their names. Massasoit was sometimes called Oosamaquin, or Asuhmequin ; though he is more generally known in history by the name of Massasoit. After him one of the Cotton Factory companies, and the largest factory building in this place, are called.

a remarkable man. Though a mere savage—ignorant of letters, even of reading and writing, and though he always resisted every effort to convert him to Christianity, and died a Pagan—yet there was an intrinsic dignity and energy in his character, which gave him unbounded influence over his subjects and inferior Sachems. The native qualities of his intellect and his heart were so commanding and so peaceful, that he gained the loyalty, controlled the extravagant passions, and secured the personal confidence of his subjects, and for nearly half a century preserved peace and harmony between them and our fathers. He was highly valued and much respected by his English neighbors, and greatly beloved by his own people. Hobomok, an Indian who became a believer in Christianity, and maintained his Christian character to the end of life, was well acquainted with this venerable chief. This Christian Indian was sent by the Governor of Plymouth, in company with Edward Winslow, to visit Massasoit, and to furnish him with medicine when he was dangerously sick. News (which proved to be erroneous) was received while on their way, that Massasoit was dead. Hobomok was greatly grieved at the intelligence, and addressing Winslow, said—"While you live you will not meet the like of Massasoit among the Indians. He was no liar, nor bloody, nor cruel like others of his race. In anger and passion he was soon reclaimed. He was easy to be reconciled toward such as had offended him. His reason was always open, and he governed his people better with few blows than others did with many." Of the year of Massasoit's death we are not certainly informed ; it probably occurred in 1661 or 1662, when his age exceeded fourscore years.

Massasoit had two sons. The name of the elder son was Wamsitta, or Wamsutta; (his earlier name was Mooanam ;) and of the younger, Metacomet, (sometimes written Metacom, and Pumetacumb.) These sons, while at Plymouth, after the death of their father, professed great friendship for the whites, and desired English names ; whereupon Governor Prince named the elder brother ALEXANDER, and the younger PHILIP ; probably from Alexander and Philip of Macedon. Alexander was the successor of Massasoit as chief Sachem of the Wampanoags, or Pokanokets ; indeed, during the latter part of his father's life, he seems to have shared his authority. He survived his father but a short period, (probably only a few months,) and was succeeded by his brother Philip, who became chief Sachem or king in 1662. Of Philip we shall speak more fully hereafter.

POCASSET was the Indian name of the territory now included in Swanzey, Somerset, Fall River and Tiverton ; and this territory was inhabited (in 1620) by the Pocasset tribe, of which Corbitant was Sachem.* At that time the Pocasset tribe was not numerous, having been greatly reduced in numbers, in common with the neighboring tribes, by the sweeping pestilence of 1612.†

Corbitant's chief residence was at Mattapoiset,‡ (now Gardner's Neck,) in Swanzey. He probably resided a part of the time at or near where this village now is. He was one of the most renowned Sachems within the dominions of Massasoit ; but unlike that venerable man, was opposed to the whites, whom he viewed as intruders, and probably designed to exterminate, if opportunity presented. His character strongly resembled that of the famous King Philip. How or when he died, we are not informed. Some have supposed that the Indian skeleton, now in the Fall River Athenæum, is that of the Sachem Corbitant.§

The successor of Corbitant, as Sachem of the Pocasset tribe, was a female—probably she was his daughter. Her name was Weetamore, sometimes written Weetamoe.‖ Her head-quarters were on the spot, as is believed, where this village is now built. She had another residence near Howland's bridge. Weetamore was twice married—first to Alexander, the eldest son of Massasoit, and after his death to Petananuet, called familiarly Peter Nunnuit. Early historians speak of her as a woman of superior intelligence, and as

---

*One of our Cotton Factory companies is called the Pocasset Company; and the principal Hotel in the place was built by said Company in 1833, and is a splendid building.

†Some have supposed that pestilence was the small pox. Be that as it may, it nearly depopulated what is now the Eastern section of Massachusetts.

‡A part of Rochester, also, was called Mattapoiset—sometimes written Mattapois.

§A human skeleton found ten or twelve years ago in the sand-bank in the southeast part of this village. This skeleton was buried in a sitting posture, and the body was found to be enveloped in a covering of coarse bark, under which, on the breast, was a plate of brass, and below this a belt of brass tubes encircling the body, and enclosing arrows of brass. Whether or not anything was engraved upon this brass plate, it is impossible, from its corroded state, to determine. The skeleton is in a tolerable state of preservation, and was evidently the body of a distinguished personage. When found, the head was only about one foot below what had been for many years the surface of the ground.

‖She was called also Namumpum and Tattapanum. The deed of Freetown, given by the Indian Chiefs, is signed by Wumsitta, (i. e. Alexander,) and a squaw named Tattapanum. I think without doubt Tattapanum was Weetamore, the Squaw Sachem of Pocasset.

"potent a Sachem as any round about her, and as having as much corn, land and men at her command." When Philip's war was approaching, he had the address to secure her countenance and aid, by insinuating (without the least reason,) that the authorities at Plymouth had poisoned his brother Alexander, her former husband. Petananuet was not concerned in Philip's war against the English, but forsook his wife, and joined them against her, and was employed with very great advantage by the whites. Weetamore having joined Philip, his fortunes became thenceforward her own.†

Having spoken of Philip's war, (as it is usually called,) it will be proper to spend a few moments upon some of the events of it which transpired in this neighborhood; especially as this place and vicinity was the seat of some of its important incidents, and also as Capt. (afterwards Col.) Benjamin Church, the leading opponent and conqueror of Philip, was for a number of years a resident at this place, and an owner of the land on which a portion of this village stands.

King Philip's talents were of the highest order. As a politician, he was the greatest of savages. He clearly foresaw that the spreading dominion of the English—their arts, their knowledge, their discipline, and their constant numerical increase, would inevitably result in the expulsion of the aboriginal race from the land of their fathers. While, therefore, he saw the whites extending their settlements over the dominions of his ancestors, in all directions, he easily kindled into resentment. Considering himself and his brethren the original proprietors and lords of the soil, he formed a plan to prevent the loss of his liberties and his country. This plan had for its object, the entire annihilation of all the whites in the land.

For several years Philip was busily engaged in enlisting the various tribes of New England in his plot, and in preparing for complete success; and had not his designs been revealed to the English, through the fidelity of two or three friendly Indians, it is not improbable that Philip's purpose would have been accomplished, and not a single white person would have been left to transmit to after ages an account of the early settlement of Plymouth Colony.

Philip's designs being discovered, the war was begun prematurely in June, 1675, by an attack upon the English at Swanzey. This

†The Indian name of Little Compton was Sogkonate, (afterwards Seaconnet, or Seconet,) and it was inhabited by the Seaconet tribe, at the head of which, when Philip's war commenced, was an influential female Sachem, named Awashonks.

war, which lasted less than two years, was of the most sanguinary and dreadful character. One of the first important battles was fought July 8, 1675, between fifteen white men under command of Captain Church, and three hundred Indians, at Puncatees, (sometimes written Puncatest,) now the South part of Tiverton. The battle was fought in and near a peas field belonging to Capt. Almy, and is called "Almy's peas field fight." The contest lasted six hours, when Church and his men, after a most desperate defence, and without the loss of a single man, were rescued from their perilous condition by a sloop commanded by Captain Golding, who approached them from a small ledgy island, a little South of Howland's bridge. The island thenceforward took the name of Gold Island, or Golding's Island, which it still retains. Church was pious as well as resolute. During the fight, when some of his men were disheartened and ready to surrender, he encouraged them by affirming "that the remarkable and wonderful providence of God, in hitherto preserving them, encouraged him to believe with much confidence that God would yet preserve them, and that not an hair of their heads should fall to the ground."

July 18, 1675, ten days after the battle at Puncatest, there was another battle with Philip and Weetamore, and their warriors, in the great Pocasset swamp, which lies a little South of this village, and stretches several miles (with now and then a solid strip of land) through the interior of Tiverton. The army of the English did not arrive until late in the day, but soon entered resolutely into the swamp. Though the first that entered were shot down, the rest rushing forward, soon forced the Indians from their hiding places, and took possession of their wigwams, about one hundred in number ; but night approaching, a retreat was ordered. The attack was desperate. Sixteen brave men, on the part of the whites, were killed. Philip and Weetamore, and most of their warriors, made their escape by crossing Taunton river, just above this village, and fleeing to the West.* About one hundred of their people were left behind, who fell into the hands of the English.

It will not comport with the design of this discourse to trace out the movements of the contending forces in other and more remote sections of New England. We can only say that the war was pros-

---

*The Indian name of Taunton Great River was Tehticut, or Titicut.

ecuted, with great courage and slaughter on both sides, till mid-summer in 1676, when the Indians were defeated in several success-ive battles, large numbers of them were made prisoners, their most valiant captains were taken or slain, and Philip himself was killed. Among the officers commanding the forces of our ancestors, Capt. Benjamin Church was prominent;—indeed as a bold, intrepid, suc-cessful fighter, he was the most prominent officer. For fifteen months he was almost constantly in pursuit of the foe, or in perilous and bloody fight. On the 31st of July, 1676, he fell upon Philip and his warriors, between Taunton and Bridgewater, and took many prisoners, among whom was Philip's wife and little son, nine years of age. Six days after, (August 6,) Weetamore, the Squaw Sachem of Pocasset, being closely pursued, was drowned in returning to Po-casset, while attempting to cross Taunton river upon a raft, at or near Slade's Ferry; and thus ended her earthly career. A few days after, Capt. Church came with his company to Pocasset, in pursuit of Philip, but not finding him here he crossed over the ferry, (now Howland's bridge) to the Island, when just at evening an Indian named Alderman, of the Pocasset tribe, arrived from Mount Hope and informed him that Philip with his warriors was in a swamp near the Mount, and that he had shot his (Alderman's) brother that afternoon for proposing to Philip to make peace with the English. Alderman offered to pilot Capt. Church to the spot where Philip was, and forthwith Church crossed Tripp's Ferry (now Bristol Ferry) with his company, and at day-light on the morning of the 12th of August, 1676, they had surrounded the swamp in which Philip was encamped. Church placed two men, an Englishman and a friendly Indian together, at suitable distances around the swamp, and sent an officer with a small party of men into the swamp to commence the attack and drive Philip and his company out. The enterprize was successful, and Philip, as he was fleeing, was shot through the heart by Alderman, whose brother Philip had killed the day before : and with him were slain several of his trustiest followers. Thus fell the celebrated King Philip.*

Never perhaps did the fall of a warrior or a prince afford more scope for solid reflection. Philip was certainly a man of great pow-ers of mind, and his death in retrospect, makes different impressions

---

*The steamboat plying regularly between this port and Providence, is called King Philip, after the Indian Sachem.

from what were made at the time of the event. It was then considered as the extinction of a virulent and implacable enemy; it is now viewed as the fall of a great warrior,—a penetrating statesman, a mighty prince. It then excited universal joy and congratulation, as a prelude to the close of a merciless war:—it now awakens sober reflection on the instability of empire, the destiny of the aboriginal race and the inscrutable decrees of heaven. The patriotism of the man was then overlooked in the cruelty of the savage, and little allowance was made for the natural jealousy of the prince, on account of the barbarities of the warrior. Philip, in the progress of the English settlements, forsaw the loss of his territory, and the extinction of his race, and he made one mighty effort to prevent the catastrophe. Had his resources been equal to those of his opponents, their ruin would have been entire. This exterminating war would perhaps never have been known to succeeding ages of civilized men.

But while we drop the tear of humanity over the destiny of Philip, the assurance of the justice and equity of our ancestors, in giving a fair equivalent for the lands purchased of the natives, is highly consoling. The excellent and upright Gov. Winslow, of Plymouth Colony, in a letter to the Governor of Massachusetts, dated at Marshfield, May 1676, says: "I think I can clearly say, that before these present troubles broke out, the English did not possess one foot of land in this colony but what was fairly obtained by honest purchase of the Indian proprietors; nay, because some of our people are of a covetous disposition, and the Indians, in their straits, are easily prevailed with to part with their lands, we first made a law that none should purchase or receive by gift any land of the Indians, without the knowledge and allowance of our court." [Vide Hubbard's Narrative.*] Thus justice was aimed at by the leaders and government of Plymouth Colony. And it is no doubt true that "our ancestors uniformly acknowledged the natives to be the right-

*Further proof of the justice and benevolence of our ancestors towards the Indians, is furnished by their self-denying labors to instruct and christianize them. The venerable John Elliot, (born 1604, died 1690,) was in his prime, and had done much for the Indians previous to Philip's war. He began to preach to the Indians, in their own tongue, as early as 1646. He once preached the Gospel to King Philip, who rejected it with disdain. He translated the Bible, and other Christian books, into the language of the Indians. An edition of his Indian Bible was printed in 1663, and a second edition in 1685. These were printed at Cambridge, and were the first editions of the Bible printed in America. Holmes (vol. 1, pp. 415, 419 of his annals) says that in 1681 there were in Plymouth Colony 1439 praying Indians, besides children, who were supposed to be three times that number; and that in 1696 "there were in New England thirty Indian churches."

ful owners of the soil; and with the exception of the Pequod country, (which was obtained by conquest,) there is the fullest evidence
that the lands in New England were obtained by fair purchase of
the natives."

Sixteen days after Philip was slain, i. e., August 28, Annawan,
his chief captain, was taken.   His capture furnishes one of the most
astonishing instances of daring intrepidity, on the part of Captain
Church, recorded in modern or ancient history.   Annawan was in a
great swamp, called Squannaconk, in the eastern part of Rehoboth,
and had with him fifty or sixty of Philip's most resolute warriors.
Church, having left his lieutenant and most of his company, was out
several miles from them, on a scout, having only one white man and
five or six friendly Indians with him.   While thus scouting, he cap-
tured an old Indian and a young squaw, who were just from Annawan's camp.   From them he ascertained the locality and condition
of Annawan.   Learning that Annawan rarely spent two nights in
one place, Church resolved to attempt to capture him that very night ;
and not having time to return to his lieutenant for his whole company, he proceeded forthwith to Annawan's retreat, with only one
white man and half a dozen friendly Indians to accompany him,—
"assuring them that if they would cheerfully go with him, the same
Almighty Providence that had hitherto protected and befriended
them, would do so still."   Before midnight he surprised Annawan*
and his warriors, and took them prisoners, without firing a gun, and
without the loss of a man.   [Vide History of Benjamin Church,
p. 131.]

Thus the death of Philip, and the capture of his chiefs and warriors, was the signal of complete and final victory.   The Indians, in
all this region, immediately submitted to the English, or fled and incorporated themselves with distant tribes.   And before the year
1676 closed, Philip's war was terminated, and with it the Indian
wars of Massachusetts proper.   It is an interesting fact that the
aboriginal inhabitants of this region contended for their supremacy,
and lost it, where just one century later the children of their con-
querors contended for independence, and gained it.

In this short but tremendous war with Philip, about six hundred
of the English—composing their principal strength—were either killed
in battle or murdered in cold blood by the enemy ; twelve or thirteen

---

*One of our Cotton Factory Companies is called the Annawan Company.

towns were entirely destroyed; and about six hundred buildings, chiefly dwelling houses, were burnt. In addition to this, an enormous debt was contracted, and most appalling sufferings were endured.

Perhaps some of my youthful hearers may ask, what became of Annawan and his principal associates? They were carried to Plymouth, and there executed by order of the government. Capt. Church remonstrated against this course, but in vain. In later times, the conduct of the government, in this particular, has been much censured,—it certainly does seem severe. But we should remember that many, very many, whole families of the English had been murdered by these very Indians, in cold blood; indeed, there was scarce a family in the Colony who had not mourned the death of one or more of its relatives, tortured and murdered by the Indians. Moreover, Annawan and others had been declared outlaws by the government, long before they were taken; and he confessed that he had put to death several of the English who were taken alive, (ten in one day,) not denying that some of them were tortured. These facts should not be forgotten in forming an opinion of the measures of the government. Still, we lament the sad end of the native heroes of the soil we now occupy, and can do it in no language more appropriate than that of President Dwight:

> " Indulge our native land, indulge the tear
> That steals impassioned o'er a nation's doom;
> To us each twig from Adam's stock is dear,
> And tears of sorrow deck an Indian's tomb."

In view of the foregoing sketch of the aboriginal history of this place and vicinity, there are three particulars in which the finger of Divine Providence is most signally manifested in the early settlement of this part of New England.

1. In removing the great body of the Indians by pestilence, six or eight years before the arrival of the first English settlers. Of the occasion of that sore judgment, we have nothing now to say. The fact is notorious. God had good and wise reasons for their removal; and their remarkable removal just at this juncture, prepared the way for the settlement of another people; herein is seen the hand of God.

2. In raising up for the first white settlers a friend so firm, so influential, so unvarying as was Massasoit, to hold the few Indians still living, in check, for nearly half a century, till the colonists had

D

felled the forests and built dwellings, and become sufficiently-strong
and numerous to act on the defensive. If the natives had continued
as numerous as they were before that pestilence, or if such a man as
Philip had stood in the place of his father, no European could have
gained a permanent foothold in New England.

3. In raising up such a man as Benjamin Church for the defence
of the Colonists, and in preserving his life amid the imminent perils
to which he was subjected. Church was certainly a wonderful man,
raised up for a most difficult service. He says himself, "through
the grace of God I was spirited for that work, and direction in it
was renewed to me day by day. Although many of the actions I
was concerned in were difficult and dangerous, yet myself, and those
who went with me voluntarily in the service, had our lives, for the
most part, wonderfully preserved by the overruling hand of the Almighty, from first to last—and to declare His wonderful work, is our
indispensable duty. I was ever very sensible of my own unfitness to
be employed in such great services. But calling to mind that God
is strong, I endeavored to put all my confidence in Him, and by His
Almighty power, was carried through very difficult actions; and my
desire is that his name may have all the praise."

At the formation of the Congregational Church in Bristol, R. I.,
1687, (in the days of Rev. Samuel Lee,) Church was a member.
He is represented by his son as constant and devout in family worship, wherein he read and often expounded the Scriptures to his
household. In the observance of the Sabbath, and in attending the
worship and ordinances of God in the sanctuary, he was exemplary.
As a warrior, he seems to have understood perfectly the best manner
of coping with the Indians; and it was in battling with them that his
success was wonderful. His surprisal and capture of Annawan and
his warriors, was an act of heroic boldness which has no parallel in
modern times.

Previous to Philip's war, Church had purchased and commenced
operations upon a plantation at Seaconet, now Little Compton. His
operations there were suspended by the war; and when it was over,
he lived first at Bristol, then at Fall River, and lastly at Little Compton, where he died and was buried. On his tomb-stone is the following inscription:

"Here lieth interred the body of the Honorable Col. BENJAMIN

CHURCH, Esq., who departed this life January 17th, 1717–18, in the 78th year of his age."

Another hand has added :

> " High in esteem among the great he stood,
> His wisdom made him lovely, great and good;
> Though he be said to die, he will survive;
> Thro' future time his memory shall live."

[See Appendix, Note A.]*

II. The Civil History.

Fall River was a part of Freetown till 1803. Hence the earlier history of our town is that of Freetown.

On the 3d of July, 1656, the General Court of Plymouth granted to sundry of the ancient freemen of that jurisdiction, namely : Capt. James Cudworth, Josiah Winslow, senior, Constant Southworth and John Barnes, in behalf of themselves and other freemen, a certain tract of land East of Taunton River, from Assonet† Neck to Que-quechan, and extending East four miles. On the 2d of April, 1659, a warrantee deed of what is now included in the towns of Freetown and Fall River, was given to Capt. James Cudworth and others, by Ossamequin, i. e., Massasoit, Wamsitta, the son and successor of Massasoit, and Tattapanum, (supposed to be the wife of Wamsitta, the Squaw Sachem of Pocasset, usually called Weetamore.) [See a copy of this deed, Note B, Appendix.] This deed was signed by Wamsitta and Tattapanum, and sealed and delivered in the presence of witnesses, and was duly acknowledged June 9, 1659. Ossame-quin never signed the deed. By some, it is supposed that he died before it was completed. That he lived a year or two later is prob-able, though not certain. If living at the time this deed was exe-cuted, he was very aged, and perhaps declined business, or commit-

---

*INDIAN NAMES OF PLACES IN THIS VICINITY. — Pocasset—Fall River and Tiverton. Seaconnet—Little Compton. Punkatees, or Punkatest—South end of Tiverton. Aquetneck, or Aquidneck, or Aquidnick, or Aquetnet—Rhode Island: which was called by the English, the Isle of Rhodes, after the Island of Rhodes in the Mediterranean, near the coast of Asia Minor; and hence Rhode Island. Poka-noket—Bristol. Keekamuit, or Kickamuit—Warren and Bristol. Mattapoiset, or Mattapois—Swanzey and Rochester. Namasket—Middleborough. Ponaganset, or Aponaganset—Dartmouth. Assawamset—Ponds in Middleborough. Cushnet, or Acushnet—River between New Bedford and Fairhaven. Tehticut, or Titacut—Taunton Great River. Sconticut—Fairhaven. Agawam—Wareham, Ipswich and West Springfield. Pappoosesquaws, or Papposquash, or Poppysquash Neck—The point opposite Bristol. Shawmut—Boston. Sowams, or Sowamsett—Somerset. Cohannet—Taunton. Mooshausick—Providence. Nannaquacut, or Quacut—A point of land in Tiverton, South of the Stone Bridge.

†Assonet is an Indian name, signifying, it is said, a song of praise.

ted it to the hands of his eldest son, Wamsitta. The consideration for this purchase is mentioned in the deed; and though it seems small at the present time, it was probably a fair price then, and was so considered by all parties. Thus it appears that the lands of Freetown and Fall River were obtained peaceably, and for a satisfactory consideration. The purchasers were freemen in the towns to which they severally belonged, and the purchase was called the Freemen's Purchase; and hence the town, when it was incorporated, was called Freetown. The first settlers were principally from Plymouth, Marshfield and Scituate. Some were from Taunton, and a few from Rhode Island. The early names were Cudworth, Winslow, Morton, Read, Hathaway, Durfee, Terry, Borden, [See Note O, Appendix,] Brightman, Chace, Davis. Freetown was incorporated in 1683.* The Freemen's Purchase was divided into twenty-six shares, and the shares were set off—whether by lot or otherwise does not appear— to the several purchasers. After the division into shares was made, there was a piece of land between the first lot or share and Tiverton bounds, which, in 1702, it was voted by the proprietors should be sold "to procure a piece of land near the centre of the town, for a burying place, a training field, and any other public use the town shall see cause to improve it for." Accordingly this piece of land was sold to John Borden, of Portsmouth, R. I., (the highest bidder,) for nine pounds and eight shillings, and was the territory on which that part of this village South of Bedford street and North of the stream now stands. This John Borden is believed to be the ancestor of all who sustain his name in this vicinity.

Tiverton (excepting a small part at the South end of the town, called Puncatest,) was purchased by a company of eight individuals, namely: Edward Gray, of Plymouth; Nathaniel Thomas, of Marsh-

---

*At the time Freetown was incorporated, there was but one county in the Colony of Plymouth. In 1685 the Colony was divided into three counties, which were called Plymouth, Bristol and Barnstable. Bristol County then comprised (in addition to the present territory,) Cumberland, Barrington, Warren, Bristol, Tiverton and Little Compton, R. I. Bristol was incorporated in 1680, and in five years became the most thriving town in Plymouth Colony. When the Colony was divided into three counties, Bristol was made the County seat, and the County was named Bristol County, in honor of the town. Bristol continued to be the County town till 1746, when it was set off, with Warren and Barrington, to Rhode Island, and those towns were made a County in that State, named Bristol County. The name Bristol was continued to what remained in Massachusetts, also, and of this portion, Taunton thenceforward became the County seat. In 1692, the three counties comprising Plymouth Colony were united with Massachusetts, and the Plymouth Colony government then terminated. In 1840, the population of that part of Massachusetts originally comprised in Plymouth Colony, was 153,121.

field; Benjamin Church, of Puncatest; Christopher Almy, Job Almy, and Thomas Waite, of Portsmouth, R. I.; Daniel Wilcox, and William Manchester, of Puncatest. The sum paid for it was eleven hundred pounds, or about $3,666. The purchase was called the Pocasset purchase. It was bounded northerly by the Freemen's purchase; westward, by the Bay; southward, partly by the Sea-connet bounds, and partly by Dartmouth, which then included West-port, and extended east from the Bay from four to six miles. It was deeded to the Pocasset purchasers by Josiah Winslow, Governor; Major William Bradford, Treasurer; Thomas Hinckley and James Cudworth, Assistants, March 5, 1680, and acknowledged March 6, 1680; recorded Dec. 19, 1723,—Bristol County,—Samuel Howland, Register. [See a copy of the deed, Note D, Appendix.]

This territory was purchased by the above grantors, of the Indian Sachems. The North end of the town was settled by Colonel Church, and the ancestors of the numerous families now in this region by the name of Borden and Durfee. The town was at first called Pocasset; and when it was incorporated, in 1694, it was called Tiverton. The origin of this name, in its application to this town, is not known. It is supposed that some of the early settlers came from a borough in Devonshire, England, called Tiverton, or Twyford-Town, lying between the rivers Exe and Loman; and that they called Pocasset after their native town, Tiverton.

For several years after Freetown and Tiverton were incorporated, there was a dispute respecting the boundary line between the two towns, which was amicably adjusted in 1700, by a committee consisting of Josiah Winslow, Robert Durfee and Henry Brightman, of Freetown; and Richard Borden, Christopher Almy and Samuel Little, of Tiverton. From their report it appears that the division line, then settled, ran by a cleft-rock, over which the store of Read & Bowen now stands, southwesterly to the Fall River, thence the River to be the bound to its mouth; and from the aforesaid cleft-rock, easterly about where Bedford street now runs. This continued to be the division line so long as Tiverton belonged to Massachusetts. [See Note E, Appendix.)

The Pocasset purchase (after reserving thirty rods wide adjacent to the Freemen's purchase and Fall River, and some other small tracts, including a tract near Howland's Bridge for house lots,) was divided into thirty shares, and distributed among the proprietors,—the lot nearest Fall River being numbered one. The piece of land thirty rods wide, adjacent to Fall River, including the water power on the South side of the River to Main street, and on both sides East of said street, extended to the Watuppa Pond, and contained sixty-six acres. This piece also was divided into thirty shares, and sold by the original proprietors. Col. Church, and his brother Caleb, of Watertown, (who was a millwright,) bought twenty-six and a half of the thirty shares of this sixty-six acres, and thereby became the chief owners of the water power. On the 8th of August, 1691, Caleb Church sold his right in this property (13 1-2 shares) to his brother Benjamin, who thus became the owner of twenty-six and a half shares. Probably John Borden, of Rhode Island, purchased the other three and a half shares. In 1703, Col. Church had moved to Fall River, and improved the water power by erecting a saw-mill, grist-mill and fulling-mill. His dwelling house* stood between the present dwelling house of Col. Richard Borden and that of his brother Jefferson, and remained till within forty years. He continued at Fall River but a few years; and Sept. 18, 1714, then living at Little Compton, sold the above named twenty-six and a half shares (his son Constant signing the deed with him) to Richard Borden, of Tiverton, and Joseph Borden, of Freetown, sons of John;' and thus the lands on both sides of the river, with all the water power, came into the possession of the Borden family as early as 1714; for, as I have before said, John Borden had previously purchased the water power on the North side of the river, West of Main street.†

As early as 1740, a dispute had arisen between the Colonies of Massachusetts and Rhode Island, respecting the Eastern boundary of Rhode Island. This dispute was made known to the King of England, who appointed commissioners to visit the spot and determine where the boundary line should run. These commissioners met, and after due examination, decided‡ that the line should be run so as

---

*There is a tradition that Col. Church first lived in a wigwam, nearly opposite the dwelling house of Capt. Joseph S. Barnard, a little West of which is a spring, formerly called Church's Spring.

†Caleb Church sold his 13 1-2 shares to his brother, for £100. At this rate, the whole sixty-six acres was valued, in 1691, at about $740. The piece on the North side of the stream cost John Borden about $31,34; total, $771,34. This included the whole of the water power and most of the land where the village now stands, together with a strip East to the Watuppa Pond. Twenty-six and a half out of thirty shares of the above sixty-six acres, were sold by Col. Church and son, in 1714, for £1,000, or about $3,333.

‡I have not been able to ascertain on what ground the commissioners made this decision, nor why the King confirmed it. All the facts in the case which have come to my knowledge, go to show that the decision was unfounded, and that Massachusetts had good reason's to be dissatisfied with it.

to include the present towns of Tiverton, Little Compton, Bristol, Warren, Barrington and Cumberland, in Rhode Island. These towns had till then been in Massachusetts. From this decision Massachusetts appealed to the King in council, who confirmed the decision of the commissioners; and in May, 1746, the King (George the II.) in council, ordered that Rhode Island and Massachusetts should appoint commissioners to run the lines, setting off the above towns to Rhode Island. Massachusetts was so dissatisfied with the decision, that she sent no commissioners on her part; but commissioners appointed by the General Assembly of Rhode Island, met and run the lines of these towns. In running the North line of Tiverton, they commenced "at the mouth of Fall River, and from thence measured 440 rods southerly on the shore, as the said shore extendeth itself from the mouth of said Fall River, and from the point where the said 440 rods reached, being East 35 degrees South of the Southernmost point of Shawomet Neck, they ran a line three miles East to the Watuppa Pond, and across said pond."‡ This line became from that time the dividing line between Tiverton and Freetown, and in consequence of it the heart of this village, including all the water power, which was previously in Tiverton, has since 1747 been in Freetown or Fall River, and consequently under the jurisdiction of Massachusetts. Tiverton being thus annexed to Rhode Island, was incorporated anew by the Legislature of that State in January, 1746 old style, or 1747 new style, and set off to Newport County; and the first town meeting in Tiverton, after it was thus set off, was held at Isaac Howland's near the bridge, Feb. 10, 1747, new style. [See Note F, Appendix.]

Previous to the commencement of the war of the Revolution, and during that conflict, the people of the towns of Freetown and Tiverton, in common with the rest of New England, took an active and patriotic part; though there were individuals here who espoused the cause of the mother country.

Thomas Gilbert, Esq., who resided at Assonet, previous to the Revolution, embarked in the cause of Great Britain, and during that conflict held the King's commission of Lieutenant Colonel. He was a leading man in the town of Freetown, and was repeatedly chosen her representative to the General Court. He was an artful and in-

---

‡Vide the Public Laws of Rhode Island; Edition 1798, p. 113.

sinuating man, and managed to keep a considerable number of families under his influence, in opposing the struggle for independence. At length, however, the success of the patriot cause compelled him to flee to Nova Scotia for safety. He owned an estate at Assonet, which was confiscated. The loss of his property here, however, was more than made up to him in Nova Scotia, where he permanently resided after the Revolution.

But notwithstanding the intrigue and opposition of Col. Gilbert, there were some true and devoted friends of the American cause in this town. In the year 1776, a town meeting was called to see if the town would instruct their representative in regard to these Colonies being declared independent. This meeting was held July 15th, of that year, and after reciting the grievances under which the community labored, thus resolved :—"We, the inhabitants of Freetown, in public town meeting assembled, for giving instructions to our representative, do in public town meeting vote and declare, and direct our representative to declare in the General Court, that we are ready, with our lives and fortunes, to support the General Congress in declaring the United American Colonies free and independent of Great Britain."* Thomas Durfee, Esq., was their representative that year, and faithfully obeyed the above instructions.

During the early part of the war which followed the declaration of Independence, Freetown (especially that part now comprised in Fall River,) and Tiverton were constantly harrassed and distressed by the enemy, several of whose ships were frequently lying in the waters of the Narragansett Bay. On the 25th of May, 1778, early Sabbath Morning, about one hundred and fifty British troops, under the command of Major Ayres, landed at Fall River, and commenced an attack upon the few people then residing here. The men rallied under the command of Col. (then Major) Joseph Durfee, and after a brave and spirited resistance, which took place near where Main street crosses the stream, repulsed the invaders, and compelled them to retreat. They left one man dead, (who was killed directly opposite where the Pocasset House now stands, and about four rods from the front door,) and another mortally wounded, and lying five or six rods further West, who soon died. When the enemy first landed, they set fire to the house of Thomas Borden, then nearly new, and

---

*See Freetown Records, Book 2, p. 126.

standing at the head of the present Iron Works Co.'s Wharf, and also to his grist-mill and saw-mill, standing near the mouth of Fall River, which were consumed. When they were retreating, they set fire to several other buildings, which were saved by the vigilance of the little Spartan band who had given them so warm a reception, and who closely pursued them in their retreat, killing one of the retreating party after they had entered their boats. The two British soldiers killed in the engagement, were buried at 12 o'clock the same day, in the same grave, near where the South end of the Massasoit Factory now stands. The head of the one was laid by the side of the feet of the other.

Much praise was due to the defenders of Fall River for their firmness and bravery in resisting and repelling five times their number. But few, if any battles were fought, during the Revolution in which so large a force was repulsed by so small a number. Through the interposing mercy of Divine Providence, not an individual of our defenders was either killed or wounded. The officer who commanded in defence of the place, still survies, and for ten years past has received a pension of five hundred and forty-two dollars a year. He is supposed to be the only surviving Colonel of the Revolutionary army.

As the enemy were retreating, they set fire to the dwelling house of Richard Borden, then an aged man, and took him prisoner. The fire was extinguished by the vigilance of the pursuers, who greatly annoyed the British in their retreat. As they were passing Bristol Ferry, the Americans fired upon them from the shore, and their aged prisoner, to avoid danger, threw himself flat upon the bottom of the boat. Those who had him in charge, insisted that he should stand up and be equally exposed with themselves. This he resolutely refused, and two men seizing him, attempted to raise him up, and while thus engaged, a shot from the Americans on shore, put an end to both their lives. Mr. Borden was soon after released on parole.

Great credit was given, also, to another individual,* who held a Captain's commission, and who still survives and is able to meet with us this day; and to many others residing in these two towns, for their unflinching fortitude and untiring perseverance in the defence of this region, as well as for the other services they rendered the country while working out her national independence.

*Deacon Richard Durfee.

E

Among the patriots of that period, the name of a native of the Pocasset tribe must be enrolled. While the British army had possession of the island of Rhode Island, in 1777, General Prescott, the chief in command of that army, quartered at a private house some distance from the main body of his troops, and was attended only by his aid-de-camp and a small guard. Col. Barton, an American officer, a native of Warren, having learned the condition of Prescott, resolved to make a desperate effort to surprise and capture him. Accordingly he embarked on the night of the 10th of July, with about forty spirited volunteers, on board four whale boats, at Warwick neck, and crossing the Narragansett, landed on the West side of the island. Securing their boats, they silently approached the house where Prescott was quartered, seized and silenced the sentinel at the door, and entering the house, took the General from his bed, and returned with him in safety to the American forces. Among those volunteers was a young, bold, nimble-footed Indian. That Indian was one of the first to seize the sentinel at the door, and was one of two that led Prescott by the arm, a captive, from the Overing house, at which he was taken.

After leaving the house, it is said, the Indian, recollecting that Prescott's sword was left behind, returned to the chamber, found the sword, and overtook the company before they reached their boats. That Indian was Daniel Page, the last male of the Pocasset tribe, the former owners and lords of the soil where we now have our homes. Page was well known and much respected by some of my hearers. Previous to his death, a member of this church and others made an effort to secure a pension for him, which he most richly deserved; but they failed for want of living witnesses to furnish the necessary proof. Page was a native of this town. He lived and died here. His death occurred in 1829, aged fourscore years; and in his decease there is an end of his tribe. Only three or four aged females survived him.

The town of Fall River was set off from Freetown and incorporated, February, 1803, by the name of FALL RIVER. The first town-meeting was called by Charles Durfee, Esq., and held April 4th, of that year, at the house of widow Louisa Borden. In 1804, the name of the town was changed to Troy, which name it retained for thirty years; when in 1834, it was changed again to Fall River. The first town house was at Steep Brook. In 1825 the town voted to erect a town house on the town land, near the dwelling house of Joseph E. Reed, Esq. This vote was carried into effect that same year. In 1836, the town voted to remove the town house to the village, which was done, and it now stands on West Central street.

Fall River is bounded North and East by Freetown; South by Dartmouth, Westport and Tiverton; and West by Mount Hope Bay and Taunton River; said River separates it from Somerset. Fall River comprises an area of about twenty-seven and four hundred and fifty-four thousandths of square miles; and of about seventeen thousand five hundred and seventy-one acres, including both land and water.* The western half of the town is rather hilly, and the land is good for farming purposes. The eastern half is of a poorer quality, and is chiefly woodland.

In the year 1823, the town purchased 4 3-4 acres of land nearly opposite the dwelling house of Joseph E. Read, Esq., and in 1830 they made an additional purchase of 3 1-4 acres, for a town burying ground, which is laid off into lots of suitable size for families, and these lots are sold at a moderate price, to all who choose to purchase. This is now the principal burial ground for the village and vicinity; though there are within the town at least twenty-one other burial places. The purchase made by the town was ready for use in the spring of 1824. Samuel Dexter Wheeler Crary, youngest son of Stephen K. Crary, born Sept. 3, 1818, fell, as he was returning from the Sabbath School, from a plank that lay across the Fall River stream, and was carried down the rocky falls, near where the Satinet Factory now is, which caused his instantaneous death. This occurred Sabbath, May 3, 1824. He was the first person buried in the town burying ground, where a great congregation have since been laid by his side.

---

*According to a survey of the boundaries of the town of Fall River in 1831, the courses and distances beginning on Tiverton line at the Bay, were as follows :

South 82 3-4 degrees	East	1,140	rods	by Tiverton line.	
South 10 3-4	"	West	132	"	" "
South 68 3-4	"	East	646	"	Westport "
North 65	"	East	1,024	"	Dartmouth line.
North 12	"	East	750	"	Freetown "
North 69	"	West	1,760	"	" "

The distance on Taunton River and Bay in a straight line, is 1724 rods. When this survey was taken, the needle varied northwesterly about seven degrees.

The following table records the number of burials, and the number of graves dug in the town burial ground by one man, (Mr. Jonathan Brightman,) for each month during the last five years :

MONTHS.	1836	1837	1838	1839	1840	TOTAL.
January, ...	0	6	3	11	5	25
February, ...	4	4	4	5	2	19
March, ...	6	6	6	6	4	28
April, ...	8	10	13	4	7	42
May, ...	5	4	6	4	13	32
June, ...	7	6	4	1	11	29
July, ...	4	8	16	7	7	42
August, ...	19	10	10	11	16	66
September, ...	16	6	10	7	15	54
October, ...	18	5	15	11	13	62
November, ...	8	6	3	5	13	35
December, ...	5	4	4	3	8	24
	100	75	94	75	114	458

Of the foregoing, in 1836, 37 were grown persons, and 63 were children; in 1837, 29 grown persons, 46 children; in 1838, 26 grown persons, 68 children; in 1839, 28 grown persons, 47 children; and in 1840, 35 grown* persons, and 79 children. Total grown persons, 155. Total children, 303.

In sixteen years, Mr. Brightman has dug about nine hundred graves, and aided in burying that number of persons in the town burying ground; and there have been interred in that ground about one hundred persons whose graves were not prepared by him; making about one thousand bodies laid already in that consecrated spot. Verily, on the morning of the resurrection it will be a spot in this town of no ordinary interest. Then the trump of God shall sound, and wake the dead; and all who lie in that field of graves shall come forth, "they that have done good, unto the resurrection of life; and they that have done evil, unto the resurrection of damnation."

During these sixteen years, about one-fourth of the burials of this population have been in the other twenty-one burying grounds in the vicinity; which, added to those entombed in the town ground, makes over 1,300 in sixteen years. If we take the last five years as a basis of calculation, eight hundred and sixty, of the whole number of deaths, were children under ten years; four hundred and forty were

*Those above ten years of age are reckoned as grown; those below ten years as children.

over ten years. Thirteen hundred deaths in sixteen years is an average of eighty-one a year. But the population has trebled in this period; and during the last five years the deaths have averaged about one hundred and sixty a year.

In view of the facts now presented, you will ask, is this a *sickly* and *dying* place? I answer, it is a *dying* place; and soon, very soon, you and I will have yielded up the ghost, and gone to stand before the bar of God. Are we prepared, through faith in the atoning blood of Jesus Christ, to go this night and give up our last account? But if you ask, is this a more sickly, a more dying place than other towns and villages in New England? I answer, no—by no means. A comparison of the bills of mortality here and elsewhere, shows that Fall River is not surpassed by any town in New England for the salubrity of its atmosphere, and the healthiness of its location.

I will speak now of the more recent history, and of the present condition of Fall River; particularly of this village. This village stands at the head of Mount Hope Bay, on both sides of the river of Fall River; and is in the South-west corner of the town of Fall River, Mass., and in the North-west corner of the town of Tiverton, R. I.; about seven-eighths of the population, and the whole of the water-power being in Mass. The River of Fall River is less than one rod in width, and about two miles in length. The Indian name of this river was " Quequechan,"* which signifies falling water, or quick running water; hence it is appropriately called Fall River. This river issues from a natural pond, called the Watuppa Pond. Watup means a boat, or the place of a boat. Watuppa is the plural form of the word, and signifies boats, or the place of boats. Fall River empties into Mount Hope Bay, nearly opposite the mount; and adjacent to its mouth is the harbor of Fall River. This harbor is easy of access, safe, and deep enough for ships drawing eighteen or twenty feet of water, to come to the wharf. The Watuppa Pond is ten miles long and about one broad. Nearly equidistant from each end of this pond, there is a narrow strait, only a few rods wide; across which lies the road to New Bedford. Within the memory of some now living, this strait (called the Narrows,) was passed on a foot bridge of stepping stones. This strait divides the pond into North

---

*One of our Cotton Factory Companies is called the Quequechan Company after the Indian name of Fall River.

Watuppa and South Watuppa. North Watuppa is supplied by several small streams, and by living springs. South Watuppa is supplied in like manner, and also by three other smaller ponds, of from one to two miles in length, one of which, called Davol pond, is in Westport, and empties into a second in Tiverton, called Sawdy pond, and this empties into South Watuppa. The other, which is in Tiverton also, and is called Stafford pond, empties by Sucker Brook into South Watuppa. These three ponds are adjacent to each other, and to the Watuppa. South Watuppa and a part of North Watuppa are in Tiverton ; the remainder of North Watuppa is in the town of Fall River.

The river of Fall River, we have said, is about two miles long ; four-fifths of this distance it is on a level with the South Watuppa, from which it issues ; and since the raising of the water in the Watuppa, within a few years, by means of the upper dam, the whole of this distance the river is much wider than the natural stream ; it is now from ten to eighty rods in width. When within one hundred and fifty rods of tide water, the river commences its fall, and descends upon an inclined plane, 132 feet. On this inclined plane, stand the factories and other buildings containing the machinery propelled by the water power, which is durable, abundant, and easily applied. This location, being adjacent to an excellent harbor, furnishes the most remarkable and most valuable combination of facilities for manufacturing and mercantile purposes in New England. It has already been remarked, that the water was improved, for grist and saw mill purposes, as early as the year 1700. For more than a century it continued to be thus improved ; and in the progress of things during that period, a few families were collected here, and found their home where we now reside. In the year 1803, when the town of Fall River was incorporated, there were, however, only eighteen dwelling houses and about one hundred inhabitants, where the village now is. In North Main street there were six houses, occupied by Charles Durfee, Daniel Buffinton, John Luthur, Abner Davol, John Cook, and Mary Borden. In East Central street there were four, occupied by Nathan Bowen, Perry Borden, Seth Borden and Elihu Cook. In West Central street there were two, occupied by Nathan Borden and Daniel Borden. In South Main street, there were five, occupied by Simeon Borden, Richard Borden, Thomas Borden, Benjamin Brayton, and Francis Brayton.

Near the shore there was one, occupied by Thomas Borden. Of these eighteen families, nine were Borden's.

The first cotton factory was built in 1813. The Troy Company and the Fall River Company were formed that year. In 1813 there were thirty dwelling houses here, and about two hundred inhabitants. From that time there was a gradual increase of the village. Still the growth, for several years, was not great. In 1820, ten respectable citizens, six of whom still reside here, had occasion to prepare a statement of facts touching the condition of this place, to be used abroad; in which they announce that "the village contains fifty dwelling houses, two large cotton factories, several stores, one large school house, several grain and saw mills, several shops for various kinds of Mechanics, and about five hundred inhabitants." It appears, also, from the census of this town, taken by order of government, that the increase from 1810 to 1820 was only 298 souls. From the year 1820 may be dated the more rapid and steady growth of the village. In ten years from that period, 2,565 were added to the population; and during the last ten years, the increase of population has been 2,579—being fourteen more than the increase of the previous ten years. The population of the town of Fall River in 1840, was 6,738, of which about 6,200 are in the village and its immediate vicinity. In 1830, the population of the town was 4,159; in 1820, 1,594; in 1810, 1,296.

In the last twenty years the population of Tiverton has increased from seven to eight hundred, nearly the whole of which increase has been in this village and vicinity. The population of Tiverton in 1840 was: white males, 1,581; white females, 1,542; colored males, 20; colored females, 40; total, 3,183. The present population of the village, in both States, reckoning all who reside within about one mile of the Post Office, which may be considered the central point, is about 7,000. Within these limits there are 537 dwelling houses* and 1,173 families. The population of the town of Fall River is, white males, 3,288; white females, 3,424; colored males, 11; colored females, 15; total, 6,738. Over ninety years old, none; over eighty, 16; over seventy, 78; over sixty, 206. The fact that only two hundred and six of our population have reached sixty years, shows ours to be a young population. Nine hundred

---

*In this statement, I reckon as dwelling houses all buildings that have families in them, and include the Bowenville and Tiverton Print Works neighborhoods. Exclusive of these neighborhoods, there are 480 dwelling houses and 1078 families.

and eighty-seven are under five years ; seventeen hundred and fifty
-seven are under ten years ; twenty-five hundred and ninety-one are
under fifteen years ; three thousand three hundred and fifty-two
(about half of the whole,) are under twenty years of age.

There are in the town, five blind persons, six insane persons, eight
idiots, and one hundred and twenty persons over twenty years of
age, who can neither read nor write, eight of whom are at the alms
house, and a large proportion of the others are Irish Catholic immigrants. There are twelve pensioners, the oldest of whom is eighty-
five years old, and the youngest seventy-six. The number of stores
and shops in the village, of all kinds, including grocers, victualers,
butchers, dry goods merchants, tailors, milliners and dress-makers,
druggists, jewelers, harness and carriage makers, house and shop
joiners, lumber dealers, painters and glaziers, auctioneers, shoe and
boot stores, barbers, blacksmiths, brass founders, &c., is 119.

The number of legal voters in the town of Fall River in 1840,
was 1,113. The number of taxable polls was 1,603 ; the number
of persons taxed, including non-residents, was 1,760. The valuation of real estate was $1,678,603 ; of personal estate, $1,310,865 ;
total, $2,989,468. The committee of the Legislature, in equalizing
the valuation for the State, have put the valuation of Fall River at
$2,552,121 ; and they have put the valuation of the whole State at
$299,878,329. In the six counties South of Boston, there are only
three towns (Roxbury, New Bedford and Nantucket,) whose valuation of real and personal estate is larger than that of Fall River,
and only eleven in the Commonwealth.*

There are in this village eight cotton manufactories, in which are
run 32,084 spindles, and 1,042 looms. About 1,370,000 lbs. of
cotton are used, and about 6,434,500 yards of cotton cloths are
annually manufactured, and 893 persons are employed. There is
one Satinet Factory, which employs 100 persons, and in which are
eight sets of cards, and other machinery sufficient to run that number of cards. In this establishment about 200,000 lbs. of wool are
used, and about 175,000 yards of cloth are made yearly.

---

*Statistics in part of Fall River, as taken by the Assistant Marshal in 1840 :—
Neat Cattle in the town, 524; Horses, 246; Sheep, 580. Value of Poultry, $1,271;
Wool sheared in 1839, 1,138 lbs. Wood sold in do., 2,814 cords. Produce of dairy,
$2,571; Produce of Orchards, $240; Hay cut in 1839, 883 tons ; Potatoes raised in
do., 14,235 bushels; Corn do., 5,554 bushels; Wheat do., 157 bushels; Barley do.,
1,609 bushels; Oats do., 1,520 bushels; Rye do., 740 bushels.

There are three Calico Printing establishments. The Fall River Print Works Company employs, on an average, 350 persons ; prints about 4,000 pieces, or 128,000 yards weekly, amounting to about 6,656,000 yards annually. The American Print Works Company employs 300 hands, and prints about the same amount yearly ; say 6,656,000 yards. The Tiverton Print Works Company employs 80 hands, and prints about 1,800 pieces weekly, amounting to about 2,994,200 yards annually. Total of Calico Prints, about 16,306,200 yards annually.

There are two Rolling and Slitting Mills, and a Nail Factory, in which are 42 machines for cutting nails, of all sizes ; and a Foundry for iron castings; owned and run by the Fall River Iron Works Company. This company employs 250 hands ; works annually about 2,200 tons of Swedes and Russia Iron ; 1,400 tons of Scrap Iron, and 420 tons of Pig and Cast Iron ; total, 4,020 tons. They use annually about 3,000 chaldrons, or 108,000 bushels of different kinds of coal. In 1840, they manufactured 38,441 casks of nails of 100 lbs. each ; or, 3,844,100 lbs. ; 950 tons of hoops, and round and square iron ; 250 tons of shapes and rods from bar iron ; and 400 tons of castings.

There are employed by the firm of Hawes, Marvel & Davol, 50 workmen in building cotton and and wollen machinery, engaged chiefly at present in building carding machines, double speeders, and Sharp & Robert's patent self-acting mules. This firm are able to turn out one mule and some other machinery weekly ; and are prepared to build any kind of machinery called for. There are about 40 hands employed in other shops in building and repairing machinery ; making a total of 90 workmen upon machinery.

There is an oil manufactory, which works 32,000 gallons of oil yearly, and employs five persons.

This neighborhood furnishes an abundance of beautiful granite, equal to the Quincy granite ; which is used in building here, and is carried to Newport, New Bedford, New York, Providence, Bristol and Warren. The business of stone quarrying and cutting, employs 30 hands ; furnishing stone, rough and hewn, worth from $10,000 to $12,000 annually, and yielding a handsome profit.*

*There is a quarry by the side of the old road to New Bedford, a mile and a half east of this village ; adjacent to which and on a platform of granite, lies a large bowlder ; a rock of the graywacke or pudding-stone formation. This rock is so

F

The total number of hands employed in the above establishments, of both sexes and all ages, is 2,093.

There are three lumber yards, in which lumber to the amount of two million feet is bought and sold yearly. The lumber is brought chiefly from Maine, and sold in this place and vicinity. With the Bowenville lumber yard, a planing machine is connected, operated by steam, which planes 1,000 feet of boards an hour.

About 1,500 tons of anthracite coal are used annually in this village and vicinity for domestic purposes. About 5,000 tons of anthracite coal, and about 8,000 chaldrons of bituminous coal, are used for manufacturing purposes.

In 1834, a marine railway was constructed to draw up steamboats and other vessels for repairing. There are five principal wharves on our shore, now in use, namely: Robeson's; the Iron Works Company's; the Steamboat Wharf, (belonging to said company); Slade's Wharf; and the Bowenville Wharf.

The steamboat King Philip, named after the famous Indian Sachem, runs regularly, and in the summer, daily, between this port and Providence.

Fall River is a port of entry. The District of Fall River embraces, besides this town, the other towns adjacent to Taunton river. From the commencement of the Federal Government to April 1st, 1837, it was called the District of Dighton, and Dighton was the port of entry. In the beginning of 1837 the name was changed, at the instance of the present Collector,* to the District of Fall River; since which, Dighton is only a port of delivery.

There are now belonging to the District of Fall River, registered, enrolled and licensed vessels, 113; in 1830 there were 50; increase in ten years, 63.

The present tonnage of the District is 8,809; in 1830 it was 4,463; increase in ten years, 4,346. Five vessels are now employed in the whale fishery, with an aggregate tonnage of 1,189; in 1830 there were none thus employed. The number of seamen employed in the District is 541; in 1830, it was 240; increase in ten years, 301. In 1839 there were foreign entries, 51; in 1830, 4; increase

poised that the pressure of a man's shoulder or hand will cause it to oscillate. Its form somewhat resembles an egg. Professor Hitchcock, of Amherst College, visited it two years ago, and ascertained its solid contents, and found its weight to be 160 tons. It may be called the Rocking Stone; and is a curiosity well worthy of a visit.

*Phineas W. Leland.

in ten years, 47. American tonnage entered from foreign countries in 1839, 10,213; in 1829, 518; increase in ten years, 9,695. Coal began to be imported from Nova Scotia, (Pictou and Sidney,) in 1833. There was imported in 1839, from Pictou, in bushels, 298,-260; from Sidney, 9,756; total; 308,016; in 1833 there was imported 98,256; increase in six years, 209,760. From 1,500 to 2,000 tons of Swedish iron have been imported, yearly, by a single firm in this town. The amount of duties collected in this District in 1833, was $13,184; in 1839, about $36,000. Increase in six years, $22,816. The average annual amount of Hospital money collected for the relief of sick and disabled seamen, is about $280.

About two-thirds of the amount of business in the District, is done in the town of Fall River. About 90 men and boys are employed in the whaling vessels belonging to this town. About 100 men belonging to this town are employed in other vessels sailing from this port, and about 200 sailing from other ports; making 390 seamen belonging to the town of Fall River. Of these, 24 are masters of vessels. In 1840, a female Bethel Society was formed for the purpose of promoting the temporal and spiritual interests of Seamen. This society has opened a room for the sale of clothing and other articles used by seamen; and gives good promise of essentially benefiting those "that go down to the sea in ships, that do business in great waters.")

A Post Office was established in this town, January 31, 1811. The first mail was opened the 12th of February following. Charles Pitman was the first Postmaster. He removed the office to Steep Brook, March 26, 1813; after which there was no post office in this village till March 18, 1816, when the present office was established, and Abraham Bowen was appointed Postmaster. He held the office till he died, April 1824. James G. Bowen, his son, succeeded him, and held the office till July, 1831, when Benjamin Anthony was appointed. He continued to hold the office till within a few days of his decease, June, 1836; soon after which, Caleb B. Vickery, the present incumbent, was appointed. The amount of postage collected at this office, for the year ending March 31, 1826, was $226.86. For the last five years the receipts have been, for postage—in 1836, $2,330.52; in 1837, $2,438.86; in 1838, $2,-669.57; in 1839, $2,960.76; in 1840, $2,956.90. The average of annual receipts at the office is $2,670.32.

There are two Banks and an Institution for Savings in the village. The Fall River Bank was incorporated in 1825, with a capital of $100,000. The capital was increased in 1827, to $200,000, and again in 1836 to $400,000, which is the present capital. The Fall River Union Bank was incorporated at Bristol, 1824, and was called the Bristol Union Bank. It was removed to Fall River in 1830. Capital, $100,000. These institutions are carefully and faithfully conducted. The "Fall River Institution for Savings" was incorporated March 11, 1828. Its object is to "provide a mode of enabling industrious manufacturers, mechanics, laborers, seamen, widows, minors, and others in moderate circumstances, of both sexes, to invest such parts of their earnings, or property, as they can conveniently spare, in a manner which will afford them profit and security." The success of the Institution has exceeded the highest hopes of its friends. It has been in operation twelve years. At the end of the first six years, $51,215 were due to depositors. The amount now due to depositors is $240,195. No person can deposit more than $1,000. The present number of depositors is 1,117. In 1840 the number of deposits was 820, and the amount was $85,294. The amount withdrawn, by 323 depositors in 1840, was $35,149 ; leaving an increase, in that year, of over $50,000. The average of dividends for the twelve years, has been six per cent. The average of dividends for the last four years, has been six and a half per cent. By means of this noble institution, thousands and tens of thousands of dollars, doubtless, have been saved to the widow and fatherless, and others in moderate circumstances, for a day of need.

In 1835 the town purchased a farm of one hundred and seventy-five acres, with a dwelling house thereon, to be improved as an Alms House establishment, for the accommodation of the poor ; since which the poor, entirely dependent, have been supported, economically and comfortably at the Alms House. The ends to be sought in providing for the poor, "whom we have with us always," are, their comfort, health, industry, temperance and moral improvement. These should be sought with economy and under such regulations as will afford all necessaries to the poor, and yet not operate as a premium upon idleness and vice. The regulations of our Alms House establishment have, thus far, in a good degree, secured these paramount ends. In 1840, one hundred and eight persons were relieved or supported; of these, sixty-three were at the Alms House, and forty-five received aid elsewhere. The average number supported at the Alms House was thirty-four, at an average cost of 72 cents per week ; twenty-five of whom were unable to perform any kind or amount of labor. Four of the number were insane ; and three-fourths of the paupers of the town, in the opinion of the Overseers of the poor, were made dependent by intemperance in themselves, or those on whom their support should have devolved. The expense of supporting and relieving the poor in 1840, including interest on Alms House establishment, was $1,800. The universal practice of the principles of Temperance, would soon reduce our pauper tax to a trifle ; a consummation which we hope may ere long be realized.

The early history of education in our community, presents a gloomy page. One hundred and twenty years ago, feeble efforts were put forth to promote common schools. A few individuals seem to have felt the importance of teaching the rising generation the knowledge of letters ; but on the other hand there is abundant evidence that, in regard to the simplest and most essential rudiments of education, for a century after the first settlements commenced, " darkness covered" this region and " gross darkness the people." In pursuing my investigations, it has been most painful to observe how often deeds and other important documents have been signed, even by individuals who had large estates, with the significent words, "his mark." I am assured by a respectable gentleman, not yet fifty years old, a native of this place, that it is within his distinct recollection that the study of English grammar was introduced into this town, and that the innovation upon established customs, as it was considered, was the subject of much conversation. Another striking indication of the state of education is seen in the fact that, so far as I can learn, only three or four persons, natives of the town of Fall River, have ever graduated at any College ; and only six or seven, including native born citizens and all who have resided here. A brighter day, however, in our educational history has dawned, and a more favorable page is being filled. In 1826, the town voted to raise $600 for the support of common schools, and appointed a General School Committee to examine teachers and superintend the schools. This measure has been annually repeated, with a gradual increase of the sum voted, till in 1840 it amounted to $4,500. [See Note G, Appendix.] Measures have been taken to divide the town into fourteen school districts, four of which are located in the village.

Most of the ten districts out of the village are necessarily small, through the sparseness of the population. Four districts in the village, embracing 1,433 children out of 1,789, (the whole number in town May 1840, between the ages of four and sixteen,) are judiciously located, and are so large that each school is classified, and each class or branch is supplied with a separate teacher—one male taking the immediate charge of the highest branch; and the general superintendence of all the branches in his district. This is an admirable arrangement, which it is hoped may be extensively adopted. [See Note H, Appendix.] Within fifteen years, nine or ten new school houses have been erected in the town, most of which are wisely constructed and judiciously located. In addition to this, seven or eight private schools are in successful operation ; and some of our youth are now in college, and others are expected soon to enter.*

In 1835, an institution called the "Fall River Athenæum," was established by the exertions of individuals, which has a library of valuable standard and miscellaneous books, amounting at the present time to 1,500 volumes, about one hundred and thirty of which are taken weekly on an average, by the proprietors, who now number over three hundred persons. Connected with the Athenæum is a valuable cabinet, consisting of specimens of common and rare minerals, shells and Indian curiosities, presented by travellers, voyagers and others.

In 1825, the printing of a weekly newspaper, called the *Fall River Monitor*, was commenced, which has sustained a respectable character and is still continued. In 1830 another weekly paper, called the *Moral Envoy*, was commenced, and continued one year. In 1832, the *Village Recorder*, a weekly paper, was commenced, and continued till 1836, when it was united with the *Monitor*. In 1837 the weekly publication of the *Fall River Patriot* was commenced, and that is superseded (within a few weeks) by the *Archetype*. Thus for fifteen years one, and for nine years two weekly newspapers have been sustained in this community. In addition to these, a large number of the principal papers and periodicals of the country are taken and read ; so that the present prosperous condition of our schools, public and

---

*The following persons, residents in this town, have graduated at College:—Nathan Durfee, at Brown University, 1824; Thomas Russell Durfee, at ditto, 1824; Nehemiah Gorham Lovell, at ditto, 1833; Lorenzo Orren Lovell, at ditto, 1833; James Nichols, at Union College, 1835; William J. Knapp, at Waterville College, 1840. The Messrs. Lovells fitted for College before their family moved to this town, and can therefore hardly be considered as graduates of Fall River.

private—together with the means of knowledge furnished by the
Athenæum, and our weekly papers, added to the fact that there are
a considerable number of learned men, in the different professions,
now resident here—shows that the educational aspect of this place
is greatly changed for the better, and that our condition now is not
below the Commonwealth at large.*

III.   The ECCLESIASTICAL HISTORY of this place, and particularly
of this Church.†

The first settlers of Freetown and Tiverton were chiefly the children of the Pilgrims, and were of the second and third generations of
those noble men.   They seem to have inherited, in some degree, the
excellent character of their renowned ancestors; yet many facts in
their history show most fully that they were not distinguished for
that superior intelligence and devoted piety which were conspicuous
in their fathers, and even in their cotemporary settlers in some of the
other towns of New England.   There are but few indications of
early efforts for the education of children; and I can find no evidence of the formation of a church of any denomination, in Freetown or Tiverton, for more than half a century after they were incorporated; nor is there any certain evidence that the people were
favored with a stated ministry, for any length of time, during that
long period.   There appear to have been a few individuals of piety,
who were anxious to enjoy the blessings of the Gospel, and of common schools; and efforts were made to procure preachers and school
teachers, and in some instances these efforts were successful, for a
limited period.   But presentments to the Court were repeatedly made
against the town of Freetown, during that period, by the grand jury,
for not being provided, according to law, with a resident ministry.
And the town, in town meeting, frequently adopted measures to
answer to these presentments, or to obtain supplies.   At a town
meeting in February, 1703, Mr. Robert Durfee was chosen agent to
endeavor to "bring in a man into town, to educate and instruct
children in reading and writing, and dispensing the Gospel to the
town's acceptance;" and the measure so far succeeded that Mr. William Way, from Marshfield, was obtained as such teacher and

*For an account of Physicians, Lawyers, Members of Congress and of the General
Court, Town Clerks, Selectmen, &c., see Appendix, Note I.

†In the delivery of these discourses, the morning and afternoon were occupied with
the Aboriginal and Ecclesiastical History, and the evening with the Civil History.
In printing, the natural order (the order in which the discourses were written,) is
adopted.

preacher, and continued his services from February 14, 1704, to January 21, 1707, when the contract between him and the town was dissolved by a vote of the town. Whether Mr. Way was ordained and installed or not, is uncertain ; probably not. After this, the town had no minister stationed among them (though they had occasional preaching,) for eight years, during which time presentments were made against the town to the Court, for living without a preacher; and in one instance, to answer the law which required that every town should have a minister, the town voted that Jonathan Dodson, one of the selectmen of the town, should be their minister; but I find no evidence that he ever officiated in this character. In May, 1709, a petition was sent to the Governor and General Court, praying for aid in settling a minister. This petition was signed by nearly twenty individuals of the town, and the General Court granted twenty pounds from the public treasury, to be paid when the minister had been here one year, provided he be a man approved by three neighboring ministers. [See this Petition, Note K, Appendix.]

In 1711, Rev. Samuel Danforth, of Taunton, on his own responsibility, took measures to supply Freetown and Tiverton with the means of grace, "lest," as he expressed it, "the noble work of gospelizing the plantations of Freetown and Tiverton should be impeded by the discontinuance of preaching among them"; and on the 15th of March, 1711, he petitioned the General Court in their favor, asking that Mr. Avery may have compensation for preaching in Freetown seven Sabbaths, which petition was granted. On the 20th of August, same year, the people of Freetown again petitioned the General Court, alleging that they had called the Rev. Recompense Wadsworth to be their minister ; and twenty pounds were granted by the General Court, on condition that a minister was settled. But objections being made against Mr. Wadsworth by some, who thought it contrary to the Gospel for a minister to have a salary, he declined the call.

On the 2d of February, 1710, the town voted to build a meeting house 36 feet long, 26 feet wide, and 18 feet between joints ; and not agreeing where to locate the said house, the town, at the same meeting, voted that Mr. Samuel Danforth, of Taunton, Mr. John Sparhawk, of Bristol, and Mr. Richard Billings, of Little Compton, should be a committee to determine where to set the meeting house ;

who came March 7th, 1710, with the knowledge and consent of his Excellency the Governor, and after due examination, determined that the house should be erected upon the land given for the purpose by the Hon. Samuel Lynde, which was in the present town of Fall River, on the east side of the road, directly opposite the dwelling house which is now owned and occupied by Capt. William Read. The reason they give for locating it there, is, that it is "near the centre of the town."* The house was completed and accepted by the town in 1714, and was thereafter used both for a meeting house and town house. It stood about one hundred years—i. e. till the year 1812 or '14—during which time it was occupied only about thirty years by a settled minister.

In 1715, Rev. Thomas Creaghead was employed as a preacher, and continued till 1721, when difficulties having arisen about his support, his labors ceased. I find no evidence that he was installed. After Mr. Creaghead's labors ceased, for twenty-five years the town was destitute of the stated ministrations of the gospel, and was considered a moral waste. During this time, presentments were repeatedly brought before the Court, because the town was not provided with a minister according to law.† The chief obstacle, all along, to the settlement of a minister, seems to have been the opposition made by a portion of the people to paying a minister a salary. At length the time arrived—Sept. 30, 1747, sixty years after the town was incorporated—when the first Church was organized. It was an Orthodox Congregational Church. Dec. 2d, of the same year, Rev. Silas Brett, of Easton, was ordained and installed as the first Pastor of the church in Freetown.‡ To the few friends of Zion in the town, and their numerous benefactors out of the town, it was a joyful day. The ordination sermon was preached by Rev. John Por-

---

*The lot upon which the house was built, was a lot of two and a half acres given to the town for a meeting house, burial ground and training field, by Hon. Samuel Lynde, of Boston.

†In 1729, when a presentment was made against the town for living without a minister, the Selectmen offered a written reply to the court, in which they say, "that they humbly conceive that no such presentment properly can be against Freetown, by reason that the lands obtained, were a free purchase without any manner of incumbrance ; and they are humbly of the opinion that the law in the case is contrary to the true intent and meaning of the royal charter, which grants liberty of conscience to all christians, papists only excepted."

‡Rev. Silas Brett was a native of Bridgewater. He received his classical education at Yale College ; though for some reason not known to me, he did not take his degree of Bachelor of Arts. He studied Theology with Rev. Mr. Anger, of Bridgewater, and preached some time at Easton, before he was settled at Freetown.

G

ter, Pastor of the fourth Church in Bridgewater, and was printed—
an imperfect copy of which I have in my possession. He speaks of
Mr. Brett in decided terms, as a sound, orthodox divine, and a man
of God, for whom the best hopes were entertained; and from his
subsequent life it seems Mr. Brett well sustained the expectations of
his brethren. The preacher speaks also of the town in the following
language : "And is Freetown to have a pastor? then let Freetown
give glory to Jesus Christ. Dearly beloved, you have been long as
sheep having no shepherd. For many years past, how melancholy
your circumstances! how dark your case! what gloomy prospects
have heretofore arisen to you and others on account of your situa-
tion and circumstances! But now, glory be to God, the sun begins
to rise on your horizon; we rejoice with you, O Freetown, that the
scene is so agreeably altered among you, and the face of things so
pleasantly changed." "These things fill our mouths with laughter,
and tongues with singing. We cannot but think, joy will diffuse
through the hearts of all that fear God and wish well to Zion, when
they shall come to hear of the transactions of this day. And the
agreeable news has doubtless reached Heaven before now, and a song
of praise has been sung by the illustrious inhabitants, to the en-
throned Jesus, on account hereof." In the preface to this sermon
the author requests "that all who have ability and a disposition to
contribute anything to so noble a purpose as the support of the gospel, and such as have the management of public collections for that
end, would remember Freetown." Says he, " I cannot but think it
would be an odor of a sweet smell unto that God who hath said,
' he that giveth a cup of cold water to a disciple, in the name of a
disciple shall not lose his reward.' "

It has already been intimated that, for many years previous to the
settlement of Mr. Brett, a portion of the people were opposed to paying a minister a salary. This opposition was so general and decided,
that before Mr. Brett's ordination, he deemed it necessary to quiet
all apprehension on this subject; and accordingly entered into an
engagement, which now stands recorded on the first book of town
records, and is as follows, to wit :

"This instrument, made at Freetown, in the County of Bristol
and province of the Massachusetts Bay in New England, this 30th
day of November, in the year of our Lord 1747, Witnesseth, that I,
Silas Brett, of Easton, in the County above said, preacher of the

gospel, and now pastor elect of the Congregational Church of Christ in Freetown above said, do hereby covenant, promise, grant, and agree to and with the aforesaid church, and the congregation usually worshipping with them, that from the day of my solemn separation to the pastoral office in said church, and for and during the full term of time of my continuance in that office, in said church, I will neither directly nor indirectly take advantage, by the laws of this province, to get a salary settled on me in the town of Freetown ; but look for and expect my support by the freewill offering of the people. In testimony whereof, I have subscribed this instrument, to be entered in the records of the church above said, and also in the records of the town, if it be desired.

Witness my hand,   ⌒SILAS BRETT."

To which is appended, on the same page of the town record, the following, to wit :

" At the motion of two of the Selectmen, we, the subscribers, do hereby manifest our assent and consent to the above written, as we are members of the imbodied Church of Freetown. Witness our hands, this first day of December, 1747,

JOHN TURNER,
SAMUEL READ,
SHADRACH HATHAWAY."

The means by which Mr. Brett was supported, were, 1st, the freewill offerings of the people, which, probably, amounted to but a trifle. 2d, a small annual grant from a Missionary Society in England, and a few friends in Boston ; by reason of which, he was to preach to a small tribe of Indians, the remains of the Pocasset tribe, east of the Watuppa pond.* 3d, the use of a parsonage house and farm—a farm given by Wm. Hall, John Turner, Ambrose Barnaby. and Samuel Read—which farm consists of fifty-three acres, and lies east of the road and adjoining thereto, in school district No. 5, of Fall River, on the North-west corner of which the school house of said district now stands—near which, some sixty or eighty rods from the road, the parsonage house formerly stood.- This farm was given April 13th, 1748, in trust to the Congregational Ministers of Dighton, Berkley and Plymouth, " for the use of the ministry, and for

---

*This tribe had a small meeting house and school house in one building, east of the north Watuppa pond, which stood till within a dozen years ; and there is a tract of about 300 acres of land there still belonging to the tribe. This is superintended by an agent appointed by the Governor and Council.

the benefit of the people in that part of the town forever.† William Hall, one of the donors, lived in Little Compton, where he was a deacon of the church. John Turner (the elder Dr. Turner) lived where Bowenville establishment now is. Samuel Read, (a Deacon of the Church) who died March 1, 1791, in the 76th year of his age, lived where Joseph E. Read, his grand nephew, now lives. Ambrose Barnaby lived half a mile North of the North line of the town of Fall River, where his grandson, Stephen Barnaby, now lives.

For about thirty years, Mr. Brett continued to labor faithfully with the people of his charge. At the commencement of the Revolutionary war, a portion of his charge espoused the cause of the mother country; and Mr. Brett, who was a firm whig, was dismissed, and removed his family to Easton. Subsequent to his dismission, he labored in several congregations; and died at Easton, April 17, 1791, aged 75. The church in Freetown, of which he had been the minister, never had another pastor. The congregation scattered, and at length the church, which was never large, became extinct. The last members have died within fifteen years. [See Note L, Appendix.]

The First Christian Society was formed in 1792, at Assonet, and built a meeting house in 1793. Elder P. Hathaway was their first minister. Thus Mr. Brett was the only settled minister in Freetown for a hundred and ten years after the town was incorporated, and his ministry occupied less than one-third of that time.

Respecting the early ecclesiastical history of Tiverton, I have obtained but few facts. From incidental notices of early writers, and from records, it seems probable that its moral and religious condition for fifty years after its incorporation, was similar to that of Freetown —being supplied only occasionally with the preaching of the gospel.

---

†The language of the deed is very explicit, and is as follows, to wit : " for the use of the ministry in the Congregational Church of Christ, gathered in Freetown the 30th of September last, and now subsisting under the pastoral care and charge of the Rev. Silas Brett, forever : provided that the said Silas Brett, the said church and their respective successors be, and remain truly Congregational, and sound in the faith ; and in case said church should by any means be dissolved, said trustees shall improve the profits and income of said house and land, for the support of some learned orthodox man in preaching the gospel in Freetown—reference being always had to the benefit of the people in the Westerly part of said town, where the present church is settled, till another Congregational Church is gathered in said part of said town." [See book 36 of Land Records at Taunton.] Such is the language of the deed ; from which it seems absolutely certain that the donors meant the avails should be appropriated forever, to that part of the town where the old meeting house stood. Yet I have lately learnt, with astonishment, that the Supreme Court of Massachusetts have decided that said parsonage belongs to a church three or four miles north, located where not one of the donors lived.

On the 20th of August, 1746, the first church was formed in Tiverton, in the South part of the town, composed of eleven men, (members of the church in Little Compton); whether there were any females or not, the records are silent. It was a Congregational Church, and continues to this day. In the preamble to the sound orthodox Confession of Faith and Covenant, adopted at the organization of the church, is this language : "It having pleased the all wise, all disposing and gracious God to shine into this dark corner of the wilderness, and to visit this dark spot of ground with the day-spring from on high, through his tender mercy, and to settle a church of Christ here, according to the order of the Gospel." On the 26th of August, 1746, the church made choice of the Rev. Mr. Othniel Campbell, of Plympton, (who had been previously ordained,) as their pastor. Whether Mr. Campbell had been previously settled at Plympton, or not, I have not learned. He was a graduate of Harvard College, in 1728. The Church invited the Selectmen to call a town meeting, to concur in the choice of Mr. Campbell, but they declined the invitation.* Mr. C. was installed Oct. 1, 1746, and preached his own installation sermon, [from 2d. Cor. vi. 1,] as was sometimes the custom at that day. His pastoral relation continued thirty-two years; when he died, Oct. 15, 1778, aged 82. During his ministry a considerable number were added to the church. After his death, a period of some twelve or fifteen years appears to have rolled around without a stated minister in Tiverton, and with only occasional supplies of the preaching of the word of God. At length, December 7, 1791, Rev. John Briggs became the stated minister of the church and people. He was dismissed October, 1801 ; when they were again destitute, except as they were supplied by missionaries, among whom were Rev. Mr. Davis, and Rev. Jotham Sewell.

In the summer of 1815, Rev. Benjamin Whitmore was ordained pastor of the church, and the next year his pastoral relation was dissolved. He has since been settled in the fourth parish in Plymouth, where he still labors with success.

Oct. 14, 1818, Rev. Ebenezer Colman was ordained pastor of the church and people, who continued with the congregation as a faithful laborer till November 26, 1823, when he was regularly and

---

*The town had previously chosen Mr. Joseph Wanton for their minister ; and though I cannot learn that he preached long with them, yet it seems the preference some of the people had for him, led them to decline uniting in the settlement of Mr. Campbell.

honorably dismissed, for the want of support. In 1825, Rev. Luther Wright statedly supplied the church and people as their minister, and continued with them three or four years, when he left them, "much beloved and highly esteemed for his work's sake."

Rev. Jonathan King commenced his labors as stated pastor Oct. 24, 1828, and continued there as a faithful and beloved servant of Christ, till 1836, when his labors ceased. Rev. Isaac Jones, the present pastor, commenced his labors Feb. 18, 1838; and May 9, the church voted to constitute him their pastor, so long as he shall continue to supply their desk. Mr. Jones is still laboring faithfully among the people. The Congregational Church in Tiverton, at no time numerous, is now composed of about forty-five members. Deacon David Tompkins has recently died, leaving a legacy to the church of about $2,000, which, with funds previously owned by them, is sufficient to enable them, with proper annual efforts, to sustain gospel ordinances constantly.

This church and society have two meeting houses, in which public worship is held alternately. The old house in the South-east part of the town, was built nearly a century since. The new house in the South-west part of the town was built about thirty years ago. If their location and the views of the people would allow of the use of one house only, it would conduce greatly to their prosperity to meet statedly, on the Sabbath, at one place.*

The first Congregational Church in Fall River was organized at the dwelling house of Deacon Richard Durfee, by a Council convened for the purpose, January 9th, 1816.† A confession of faith and form of covenant was adopted, embracing the leading evangelical doctrines of grace and rules of christian fellowship, taught by the apostles and advocated by the reformers of the sixteenth century, and by the orthodox Fathers of New England. The church, when formed, was composed of five members : Joseph Durfee and his wife Elizabeth Durfee, Richard Durfee, Benjamin Brayton, and Wealthy

---

*There is a Baptist Church with a meeting house in the South-east part of Tiverton, which has existed some seventy years. There is also a Baptist Church and a meeting house, built in 1807 or '8, near Howland's Bridge ; both of which have been supplied with pastors a large portion of the time. There is also a Friends' meeting house, with a small Congregation, half a mile north of the Bridge. But I regret that I have not obtained any very definite and full information of either of these congregations.

†The council was composed of the following ministers, to wit :—Rev. Mace Shepherd, Little Compton ; Rev. Thomas Andros, Berkley ; Rev. Sylvester Holmes, New Bedford ; and Rev. Benjamin Whitmore, Tiverton.

Durfee, the wife of Charles Durfee, Esq. Elizabeth Durfee died
May 19th, 1817, aged 63 years to a day. Benjamin Brayton died
Dec. 9th, 1829. Leaving no children, he bequeathed the most of
his property to this church, to be held in trust by the Deacons as a
permanent fund for the support of the ministry.* The other three
original members still survive, and two of them are present with us
this day. For about seven years after the church was organized,
they had neither a house for public worship, nor a settled pastor.
But from the time of their organization, they met regularly on the
Sabbath for public worship. When they were destitute of preaching, they read sermons and conducted the devotional exercises themselves, and evidently enjoyed the presence and favor of the Holy
Ghost ; and being of one heart and soul, were comforted and multi-
plied. A portion of the time (probably more than two-thirds of it,)
they had preaching through the aid of Missionary Societies ; to
which were added their own yearly contributions. The missionaries
by whom they were supplied, were the Rev. Messrs. John Sanford,
James Hubbard, Amasa Smith, Reuben Torrey, C. H. Nichols, Cur-
tis Coe, Samuel W. Colburn, Moses Osborne, Isaac Jones, Seth
Chapin, Silas Shores, Otis Lane and Loring D. Dewey ; and perhaps others, whose names I have not ascertained. During that period, a Sabbath School, of more than 100 persons, was gathered and
conducted by members of the church ; and a Benevolent Society,
composed of self-denying and devout women, was formed and went
into active operation, whose great object was to collect pupils for the
Sabbath School, and to provide clothing for all that needed help.
This Society still exists, and labors with all the freshness and vigor
of its earliest days. It has won and wedded many to the Sabbath
school, clothing them when necessary, and doing it by their own
weekly manual labor ; and some of those thus won and wedded to
the school, and clothed with bodily garments, have been won and
wedded to Jesus Christ, and clothed with the garments of salvation.
Among them is a young man lately licensed to preach the Gospel,
and now professor of the Greek and Latin languages in one of our
most prominent American Colleges. Verily, upon this sister band
will come the blessing of souls ready to perish. They will not be
forgotten before Him who promises that he who " gives a cup of cold
water only, in the name of a disciple, shall in no wise lose his re-

*This fund now amounts to about $4,000.

ward." But though the church were without a house and without
a settled pastor, they were not without a refreshing from the presence of the Lord. During the first three years after their organization, there were added to the church, chiefly by profession, thirty
members, among whom were only four males. Of these four brethren, three still survive. The other was Thomas R. Durfee, a son of
one of the five original members. This excellent young man, pant-
ing for knowledge and for the blessedness of proclaiming a Saviour's
love to his perishing fellow men, pursued a course of classical study,
and graduated with reputation at Brown University in the year
1824, after which he read theology in a regular course at Andover,
was licensed to preach the Gospel, and went to Missouri as a missionary. There he found a field of usefulness, to the cultivation of
which his intellect and his heart were admirably adapted. And
though his ministerial career .was short, it was bright and blessed.
In his preaching, his pastoral labors, and his daily life, he seems
with Paul "determined to know nothing but Jesus Christ and him
crucified." He died at St. Charles, Missouri, July 15, 1833, aged
32 years, greatly lamented, both by the friends of his youth in his
native place, and by a numerous circle at the West.

While this church was without a house for public worship, their
meetings were held sometimes at private houses, sometimes in a large
store-room, sometimes in the only school house in the place, and occasionally in the line meeting house, an edifice placed on the line
between the States of Massachusetts and Rhode Island, and erected
in 1798, by the various denominations living in the region in both
States, as a house common to all, controlled by none.

Being greatly tried for the want of a place for public meetings,
the church, early in 1819, after much reflection and prayer, took
incipient measures for building a house of worship. They were few
and feeble; they were in the midst of a people, many of whom
"feared not God," nor regarded his Sabbaths, nor his ordinances;
but weak as they were in men and means, they trusted in the Lord,
and resolved to proceed to erect a house, where they and their
children might meet to pay their vows. At that time there was not
a house for public worship, for any denomination, in the town of
Fall River; nor had there ever been one since the town was incorported in 1803, except the shattered remains of the old house built
in 1714, and standing within a few rods of the north line of the

town, which were not entirely removed till about the year 1812 or
'14 ; and the Indian meeting house east of the North Watuppa pond.
The first measure pursued by the church, was to see how much could
be raised among themselves, which did not exceed $600. Their
next step was to make known their condition to benevolent individuals and wealthy churches abroad. From this latter source, they
ultimately realized about three hundred dollars. With these scanty
means, (two years having been consumed in preparation,) they proceeded, in 1821 and '22, to the erection of a neat, commodious
House of Worship, 45 feet in length by 36 feet in breadth, with a
vestry underneath, which was dedicated in February, 1823.* This
was the second meeting house built in Fall River—the Friends having built a small house for worship in 1821.

An Ecclesiastical Congregational Society was formed in 1820,
and incorporated by the Legislature, February 1821.† The church
and society being organized, and furnished with a sanctuary, har-
moniously united in the call of their first pastor, the Rev. Augustus
B. Reed, who was ordained and installed July 2d, 1823.‡ The salary voted to Mr. Reed was four hundred and fifty dollars a year.
At the time of his settlement, the church was composed of about 35
members. During his ministry of two years and one month, there
were eleven added to the church, principally by letter. Mr. Reed
was dismissed in regular standing, August 3d, 1825. He again settled July 19th, 1826, in Ware, Mass., where, during twelve years
he labored faithfully and successfully ; and closed his life serenely,
Sept. 30, 1838, aged 39 years.

After the dismission of Mr. Reed, this people were destitute of a
pastor till the autumn of the following year, when the Church and
society presented a unanimous call to the Rev. Thomas M. Smith to
become their pastor, offering a salary of $600.‖ He accepted the
call, and was installed November 1st, 1826.§

---

*Rev. Samuel Austin, D D, of Newport, preached the dedication sermon.

†The excitement which arose in the town in consequence of this act of incorporation, soon spent itself by its own warmth, and ultimately did no harm to this Society.

‡Mr. Reed was the son of Dea. Elijah Reed, of Rehoboth. He graduated at Brown
University, 1821, and studied Theology in his native town, with Rev. O. Thompson.

‖Mr. Smith is the son of Rev. Daniel Smith of Stamford, Conn., and graduated
at Yale College, 1816. He studied Theology at Andover, and was settled at Port-
land, Me., previous to his installation here.

§I have not been able to obtain a list of the members of the Councils that installed
Messrs. Reed and Smith.

Soon after Mr. Smith's ministry commenced, the Lord in great mercy revived his work among this people, and in 1827, fifty-nine were added (principally by profession) to the church. His ministry continued four years and a half, during which eighty-nine were added to the church. Having received a call to the Church in Catskill, N. Y., Mr. Smith was dismissed in good standing, April 27th, 1831. In 1839, he was dismissed from Catskill, having received a call to the North Congregational Church in New Bedford, of which he is now the colleague pastor.

In 1827, the first year of Mr. Smith's ministry, an addition of twenty-five feet was made to the length of the meeting house.

Only two Sabbaths passed after Mr. Smith's labors closed here, before the labors of the present pastor commenced, May 22d, 1831. To him also the church presented a unanimous call to settle with them in the ministry, with the offer of a salary of $700,‡ which was accepted, and his installation took place July 7th, 1831.|| In the call and settlement of each of their pastors, the Church and Society have acted as distinct and separate bodies, (the church acting first;) and yet they have harmoniously co-operated, and deserve commendation for their unanimity, and their uniform adherence to sound, protestant, congregational principles.

In the fall of 1831, the Holy Ghost was poured again upon this flock, and before the year 1832 closed, sixty-one (ten by letter,) were added to the church. The congregation having out grown the first house of worship, this sacred Temple was erected in 1831 and '32. Its length (including the Portico) is eighty-five feet, its breadth sixty-five. On the lower floor there are 118 pews. The cost of the house and lot (not including the organ)* was about $16,000. This house was dedicated to God, the Father, Son and Holy Ghost, Nov. 21st,

---

‡In 1834, $200 were added to the salary, and $100 more in 1836.

||The Council called for the Installation of the present Pastor, was composed of the following Bishops and delegates :—*Bishops*—Rev. Erastus Maltby, of Taunton, (who offered the first prayer); Rev. Abel McEwen, of New London, (who preached the sermon); Rev. Thomas Andros, of Berkley, (who offered the installing prayer); Rev. Samuel Nott, D. D., of Franklin, Ct., (who was moderator and gave the charge); Rev. Thomas T. Waterman, of Providence, (who gave the right hand); Rev. Richard S. Storrs, of Braintree, (who addressed the people); Rev. Preston Cummings, of Dighton, (who offered the last prayer); Rev. Alvan Cobb, of West Taunton, (who was scribe); and Rev. Stetson Raymond, of Freetown. *Delegates*— C. Godfrey, Andrew M. Frink, Deacon J. Cady, Asa French, Deacon G. Babbitt, Lorenzo Lincoln, Deacon Benjamin Burt of Labanon, Conn., Amos Fowler of Rehoboth, and Deacon Elijah Reed.

*The organ was built by the Messrs. Hooks, of Boston, in 1835, and cost about $2,000.

1832 ; on which occasion the pastor preached from Haggai, 2d chap., 9th verse, and was assisted in the devotional services by several of his brethren in the ministry.

In 1834 the work of the Lord was once more revived, and during that year forty-nine were added to the church. Again in 1836 the Holy Spirit descended with great power, and during that year one hundred and nine were added to the church. In the beginning of 1840, God visited this people once more with the special effusions of his spirit, and during that year sixty-seven, all but two by profession, were gathered into the church. Thus since the first of January, 1827, there have been five seasons of special revival in this congregation, and three hundred and thirty-six have been added to the church since the installation of the present pastor. Since July, 1831, the sacrament of the Lord's Supper has been administered fifty-eight times ; at forty-five of which additions have been made to the church. Days for prayer and fasting have been set apart repeatedly by this church, from its earliest years to the present time ; and the great head of the church has evidently put his blessing upon these seasons. The wonders which the grace of God has wrought in behalf of this flock, are too many to be recounted in this brief sketch, and yet they are too great and mighty to be passed unnoticed. Verily the arm of the Lord hath been revealed in the midst of us ; and the language of the prophet, "a little one shall become a thousand, and a small one a strong nation ; I the Lord will hasten it in his time," is applicable to the history of this congregation. Let us set up our Ebenezer stone to-day, as did Samuel the prophet, saying, "hitherto hath the Lord helped us." And let us never fail to utter the cry of David, "Not unto us, O Lord, not unto us, but unto thy name, give glory, for thy mercy and thy truth's sake."

The whole number received to this church, is, original members five ; previous to Mr. Reed's installation, thirty ; during his ministry, eleven ; during Mr. Smith's ministry, eighty-nine ; since the present pastor's installation, three hundred and thirty-six ; total, four hundred and seventy-one. Of the whole number, twenty-three only (if I am correctly informed) have died. Eighteen have died since July, 1831 ; most of them firm in the faith of Christ, and with hopes full of immortality. About eighty have received letters of recommendation and become connected with churches to which they have removed ; four have been excommunicated ; and three hundred and sixty-four are now members; about forty of whom are non-residents.   There are now about two hundred and seventy families connected with this congregation.   I have baptized one hundred and fifty-eight adults, and one hundred and fifty-three children, total 311.   Fifty adults and eighty-six children were baptized by my predecessors.   Total baptisms four hundred and forty-seven. Since my connection with this people, I have married one hundred and twenty-eight couple, an average of about 13 couple a year.*

During the last ten years, the other evangelical churches in this place have shared largely also in the effusions of the Holy Spirit ; and though I am not able to state the definite number of hopeful conversions to God in this village within this period, I think it may safely be estimated at more than one thousand.   "What hath God wrought!"

It has already been mentioned that a Sabbath School was organized in the early years of this church.   This Institution has been continued, with growing numbers and increasing usefulness to the present time ; and during ten years past, it is not recollected that the Sabbath School has failed of being assembled for a single Sabbath ; nor has the pulpit been unsupplied for a single half day, in that time. In the summer of 1840, the number actually present at the Sabbath School, at one time, exceeded five hundred.   And the average number present, during the summer of that year was from four to five hundred.   The whole number belonging to the school in 1840, was about six hundred and fifty.   The instructions given in the school, have been greatly blessed of God.   In every revival with which this people has been visited, the Sabbath School has largely shared. Nearly half of those added to the church in 1840, were previously members of the Sabbath School.   A similar remark applies to all previous revivals.   We hope the time is near, when the whole congregation, indeed the whole community, will be connected with the Sabbath School.

In this sketch of our Ecclesiastical History, I must not omit a brief notice of the early benefactions of others bestowed upon this people, nor of the later benefactions of this people bestowed upon others.   Mention has already been made of early aid from Missionary Societies.   In 1817 the Mass. Missionary Society voted $80 ;

*For several years past, the annual number of marriages in this town, has been about sixty-five couple.

in 1818, $64; in 1819, $100; in 1820, $96; in 1821, $48; and in 1822, $80. For a number of years aid was received from the avails of the parsonage formerly occupied by Rev. Mr. Brett, amounting in all to about $500. In July, 1822, the Society for promoting christian knowledge, offered this church $500, on condition that they would settle a minister. The offer was at first declined, but the next year, on the settlement of Mr. Reed, was accepted; and for two years, a proportional part of that sum was received. As Mr. Reed was then dismissed, I am unable to determine whether the remainder was received or not. In the years 1826, '27, '28 and '29, $100 a year were received from the Massachusetts Missionary Society. After this the church and society were able to stand alone. Thus for ten or twelve years the pecuniary resources of this church and congregation were supplied in part by the friends of Home Missions abroad; without which the ordinances of the Gospel, in all probability, would not have been sustained in this congregation, and for which many thanks are due to God, and the benevolent who afforded their timely assistance. Since 1829, no aid has been received from abroad; but on the other hand aid has been freely, I may say liberally, imparted to others. In 1832, the church voted to make collections six times a year, i. e. once in two months, for the various prominent objects of benevolence, to wit: Foreign and Home Missions, the Sabbath School, Tract, Bible, and Education Societies. The following year the vote was repeated, and at length this was settled as the course of annual operations; and in every instance, when the time has arrived for an effort in behalf of a particular cause, a collection has been made, and usually with good success. And I believe it may be truly said that many among us are cheerful benefactors, and have learned "that it is truly more blessed to give than to receive."*

Since this church was organized, eight brethren have sustained the office of Deacon, all of whom still survive, and all but two of whom were inducted into office according to Apostolic rule, by prayer and the laying on of hands.† Five of them, having removed

---

*Within ten years this church and congregation have contributed to various objects of christian benevolence more than four times the amount of all the aid they ever received while in their weakness.

† The names of the deacons are as follows :—

from town, resigned their office, and there are only three deacons of the church at the present time.‡

In 1820, I have before stated, there was no meeting house in this village, except the one which stood on the State line. That has since been taken down, and eleven others have been erected, three of which, having been found too small, have been converted to other uses. Eight of the eleven are still in use ; most of them are large, and all of them are neat, substantial, commodious structures for public worship.

There are now in this village eleven congregations. The statistics of their history will be given, on the authority of their own ministers, or other leading members.

The Friends commenced public worship here in 1819. Benjamin Buffington, who is one of our oldest citizens, was then and continues to be their minister. Their first meeting house was built in 1821. It was removed, and their present house was erected in 1836. They have one hundred and thirty-four members, and forty families.

The statistics of the Congregational Church and Society having been already given, need not be repeated.

The Baptist Church was organized in 1781, and was located at the Narrows, two miles East of this village, where their first meeting house stood. It was called the Second Baptist Church in Tiverton, till 1825, when the church and congregation removed to the village, since which the church has taken the name of the First Baptist Church in Fall River. Their first meeting house in the village was erected in 1828, and occupied till last year, when their present house was built, and dedicated Sept. 16, 1840. They number 275 families, and 603 communicants ; a portion of their communicants reside in the region around this village. Their Society was incorporated June 1831. They have enjoyed the labors of four regular pastors : Rev. Messrs. Amos Burroughs, Job Borden, Brad-

	ELECTED.	RESIGNED.
Sylvester C. Allen,	October 17, 1821,	March 16, 1835.
Richard Durfeee,	December 1, 1823,	
Mathew C. Durfee,	August 19, 1833,	Sept. 19, 1836.
Benjamin S. Bourne.	December 16, 1833,	May 19, 1834.
David Anthony,	October 20, 1834,	
Samuel L. Whipple,	August 15, 1836,	Nov. 3, 1839.
Leander P. Lovell,	August 15, 1836,	
Philip R. Bennett,	November 14, 1836,	Sept. 18, 1837.

‡It is a noticeable fact that no Deacon of this church has departed this life ; and also, that no minister of our denomination, nor, so far as I am informed, of any denomination, has died in the town since it was incorporated.

ley Minor, and Asa Bronson, the present pastor. They have had two assistant pastors, Messrs. James Boomer and A. A. Ross, both of whom were assistants to Mr. Borden, who was entirely blind for forty years, and during his whole ministry. Their Sabbath School in the village numbers 617 ; the average attendance in 1840, was 415.

The Methodist Church was formed in 1826. Their first meeting house was built in 1827, and dedicated in December of that year. Their present house was built in 1839, and dedicated in February, 1840. Their Society was incorporated January, 1839. They have had eleven ministers, namely: Rev. Messrs. N. B. Spalding, E. T. Taylor, E. Blake, D. Webb, I. M. Bidwell, S. B. Hascall, M. Staples, J. Fillmore, H. Brownson, P. Crandall, and J. Bonney, their present pastor. They number 225 communicants and 100 families. Their Sabbath School numbers 220, and the average attendance for 1840, was about 160.

The Christian Church was organized April, 1829. Their house was built in 1831, and dedicated September 26th of that year. Their Society was incorporated June 1831. They have had eight ministers, to wit: Rev. Messrs. Joshua V. Himes, Benjamin Taylor, H. Taylor, James Taylor, Simon Clough, Mr. Lane, A. G. Cummings, and Jonathan Thompson, who has left within a few days. The number of members in full communion is 426, and of families, 140. Their Sabbath School numbers 264, and the average attendance for 1840, was 170.

The Unitarian Society was incorporated March, 1832. They purchased and occupied the meeting house formerly belonging to the Congregational Church ; and their first minister, Rev. George W. Briggs, was installed Sept. 24, 1834. He was dismissed November, 1837. Rev. A. C. L. Arnold was installed March 23, 1840. Their present meeting house was built in 1834, and dedicated January 28, 1835. Their present number of communicants is thirty, and of families ninety-five. Their Sabbath School numbers 100, and the average attendance for 1840, was 50.

The Episcopal Church was organized July 15, 1836, and is called "The Church of the Ascension." Their Society was incorporated in 1837. Two ministers have labored statedly with them,—Rev. P. H. Greenleaf, and their present minister, Rev. George M. Randall, whose labors commenced July, 1838. They have purchased the house lately occupied by the Baptist Church, which was conse-

crated August, 1840. They number 60 members in communion, and
40 families. Their Sabbath School has 130, and an average attendance of about 100.

The Associate Presbyterian Church was organized in August,
1837. They have no minister, and no meeting house, and for some
time past have discontinued public worship, or met only occasionally.*

The Catholics, who are chiefly Irish immigrants, have a house for
worship, which was built in 1836–7. They number about 110 families, and from 200 to 220 in their Sabbath School.

In March, 1840, a Universalist Society was formed, belonging to
which are 27 members, 35 families, and 35 Sabbath School teachers
and pupils. They have no school in the winter. No church is
formed. They have had preaching the year past, but now they have
no stated preacher, and no meeting house.

There are three families residing here, who are connected with the
New Jerusalem Church in Bridgewater. They commenced holding
meetings at a private house in 1839, and still continue them.

Thus while three or four of the Congregations in this village are
small, most of the others are large; and they are composed of a
young, intelligent and enterprising population. From the foregoing
statistics, it appears that the number of members, in eight of the
churches, is one thousand eight hundred and seventy-five; and that
the number of families nominally connected with the eleven congregations, is one thousand one hundred and ten. This is nearly equal
to the whole number of families in the village and vicinity. Most
of the families among us consider themselves as nominally connected
with some congregation; though many, (it is believed not less than
200 families,) rarely, if ever attend public worship.

It appears, moreover, that 2,281 are enrolled in the several Sabbath Schools, and that the aggregate average attendance in them is
1,573.

It may be added, that though this people are divided into so many
sects,—each of which is neither slow nor timid to assert and defend
its distinctive doctrinal peculiarities,—yet perhaps there is no town
in New England where more general harmony prevails, or kinder
neighborhood intercourse is enjoyed, or where the members of different denominations shake hands more cordially.

---

*This Church was subsequently disbanded.—PUB.

It is time to close this discourse. My brethren and friends, all earthly things are changing, fading, vanishing away. One generation goeth, and another cometh. "Our fathers, where are they?" We shall presently follow them, and our children, in turn, will soon lie quietly in the dust, by our side. In a little while we shall walk these streets and meet in these temples no more.

I have spoken of the origin, progress, present condition, and people, of this new and thriving place. But notwithstanding these ever falling waters, and these granite buildings, and all this iron machinery, and every thing that looks so strong and permanent around us, the time may come when this village shall be razed from its deepest foundations. Where are the people of former ages? They all sleep in the dust. Where are the mighty works which their enterprize and industry produced? They have long ago tumbled into ruin. Where is Babylon, "The glory of the Chaldees' excellency," with her broad walls and lofty terraces? Where is No, [Thebes,] populous No, with her hundred gates and her temples of massy stone? Where is Ninevah, that exceeding great city, of three days' journey about, with her 1,500 towers, 400 feet in height? They are gone, gone forever; and the spots where they respectively stood are hardly known. And what shall be the future history of this, our village? Who can ask this question? Who of us can anticipate the answer to this question, without deep solicitude? For myself, I may be allowed to say, that having spent nearly ten years of my life on this spot, and in devoting my best energies to the service of this people, I feel an interest in the future prosperity and glory of Fall River, felt for no other place on earth.

In conlusion, then, let me urge my beloved brethren and sisters in Christ, and the whole people of my charge, and all my respected neighbors of other congregations, "to fear God and keep his commandments." If the Lord be honored; if his Sabbaths be kept holy; if his word be studied and obeyed; if profanity, and intemperance, and injustice, and all immorality be put away, and truth, and purity, and piety prevail; if the family altar be set up and kept up in our houses; if our fathers and mothers, following Jesus Christ and him crucified,

"Allure to brighter worlds, and lead the way;"

if our "young men and maidens" seek the Lord, and praise His name; if our children are "trained up in the way they should go,"

I

and consecrate the dew of their youth to Him who requires the heart; then this village will grow, and live, and be the blessed dwelling place of many generations yet unborn. And, beloved, we will cleave to the precious and consoling assurance that God, who has shown us that he is rich in mercy, will yet pour forth more copious showers of grace; and that every soul in this place may be turned "from the error of his ways to the wisdom of the just." You will join me in the prayer, that those who are in infancy and youth, and all who shall rise up in our places, when we are dead and in the dust, may serve God with greater zeal and fidelity than we have done; and that the bright sun, which shall not go down for a thousand years, may rise early and shine without a cloud upon this our goodly heritage. Then, when we are gone, men more devoted to the interests of truth and piety will occupy our places, and more fervent prayers than ours will ascend from this favored spot. Then these little elms,* that now wave in the breeze, will spread their majestic branches over a people whom the King of Zion will delight to honor. Then the thousands of Israel, while they bow before the throne of mercy, with a fervor of faith and devotion kindled by the full beams of millenial glory, will here dwell in harmony and love, and divine influence will come upon Fall River "as the dew of Hermon, and as the dew that descended upon the mountains of Zion, where the Lord commanded His blessing, even life forevermore."

---

*Main Street was set with two rows of elms in 1840.

APPENDIX.

NOTE A—PAGE 19.

A late writer, speaking of Col. Church, says:—"Of all the English who bore commands during the great Indian war, none was so much feared, so much respected, and finally so much beloved by them, as this terrible and triumphant enemy. In conducting such wars, he was unrivalled; though many have acquired much reputation for their skill in managing and fighting Indians, none have exhibited a genius or an aptitude equal to Church. Anthony Wayne and Andrew Jackson have received their full share of fame for their skill and their knowledge in directing the operations of this, the most dangerous and dreadful of all the modes of war; but they were never placed in such perils and difficulties as were encountered and overcome by Benjamin Church."

Benjamin Church was born at Duxbury, 1639. He married Alice Southworth, grand-daughter of the distinguished wife of Gov. Bradford,—by whom he had five sons and two daughters. The wife of the late Deacon Sylvester Brownell, of Little Compton, was his great-grand-daughter.

NOTE B—PAGE 19. DEED OF THE FREEMEN'S PURCHASE.

"Know all men by these Presents, that we, Ossamequin, Wamsitta, Tattapanum, natives inhabiting and living within the government of New Plymouth, in New England, in America, have bargained, sold, enfeoffed and confirmed unto Capt. James Cudworth, Josiah Winslow, Constant Southworth, John Barnes, John Tesdale, Humphrey Turner, Walter Hatch, Samuel House, Samuel Jackson, John Damon, Mr. Timothy Hatherly, Timothy Foster, Thomas Southworth, George Watson, Nathaniel Morton, Richard Moore, Edmund Chandler, Samuel Nash, Henry Howland, Mr. Ralph Patridge, Love Brewster, William Paybodie, Christopher Wadsworth, Kenelme Winslow, Thomas Bourne, John Waterman, the son of Robert Waterman; and do by these presents bargain, sell, enfeoff and confirm from us, our heirs, unto James Cudworth, Josiah Winslow, &c., and their heirs, all the tract of upland and meadow lying on the easterly side of Taunton river, beginning or bounded toward the South with the river called the Falls, or Quequechand, and so extending itself northerly until it comes to a little brook, called by the English by the name af Stacey's Creek, which brook issues out of the woods into the marsh or bay of Assonet, close by the narrowing of Assonate Neck, and from a marked tree near the said brook at the head of the marsh, to extend itself into the woods on a northeasterly point four miles, and from the head of said four miles on a strait line southerly until it meet with the head of the four mile line at Quequchand, or the Falls aforesaid; including all meadows, necks, or islands lying and being between Assonate Neck and the Falls aforesaid, (except the land that Tabatacason hath in present use,) and all the meadows upon Assonate Neck, on the South side of the said Neck. And all the meadow on the westerly side of Taunton river from Taunton bounds round until it comes to the head of Weypoyset river; in all creeks, coves, rivers, and inland meadow not lying above four miles from the flowing of the tide in; and for the consideration of twenty coats, two rugs, two iron pots, two kettles and one little kettle, eight pair of shoes, six pair of stockings, one dozen of hoes, one dozen of hatchets, two yards of broadcloth, and a debt satisfied to John Barnes, which was due from Wamsitta unto John Barnes before the 24th of December, 1657; all being unto us in hand paid; wherewith we, the said Osssamequin, Wamsitta, Tattapanum, are fully satisfied, contented and paid, and do by these presents exonerate, acquit, and discharge [here all the grantees are again named] they and either of them and each of the heirs and executors of them forever. Warranting the hereof from all persons from, by, or under us, laying any claim unto the premises from, by, or under us, claiming any right or title thereunto, or unto any part or parcel thereof, the said [grantees] to have and to hold to them and their heirs forever, all the above upland and meadow as is before expressed, with all the appurtenances thereunto belonging, from us, Ossamequin, Wamsitta, and Tattapanum, and every of us, our heirs, and every of them forever, unto them, they, their heirs, executors, administrators and assigns forever, according to the tenure of East Greenwich, in free soccage, and not in capite nor by knight's service.

Also, the said Ossamequin, Wamsitta, and Tattapanum, do covenant and grant that it may be lawful for the said [grantees] to enter the said deed in the Court of Plymouth, or in any other court of record provided for in such case; in and for the true performance whereof, Ossamequin, Wamsitta and Tattapanum have hereunto set our hands and seals, this 2d day of April, 1659.

(S.)

WAMSITTA, his X mark.   (S.)
  TATTAPANUM, her X mark.   (S.)

Signed, sealed and delivered in presence of

THOMAS COOKE,
JONATHAN BRIGD,
JOHN SASSAMON.

Ossamequin never signed the deed. It was acknowledged June 9, 1659, by Wamsitta and the Squaw Tattapanum, before Josiah Winslow and Wm. Bradford, Assistants."—[*Vide Baylies' History of Plymouth, vol. 2d, part 4, p. 67.*

NOTE D—PAGE 21.

The following is a copy of the grand deed of POCASSET—now Tiverton:

"To all to whom these presents shall come, Josiah Winslow, Esq., Governor of the Colony of New Plymouth, Major Wm. Bradford, Treasurer of the said Colony, Mr. Thomas Hinckley and Major James Cudworth, Assistants to the said Governor, send Greeting; and whereas we, the said Governor, Treasurer and Assistants, or any two of us, by virtue of an order of the General Court of the Colony aforesaid, bearing date November, A. D. 1676, are impowered in the said Colony's behalf to make sale of certain lands belonging to the Colony aforesaid, and to make and seal deeds for the confirmation of the same, as by the said Order remaining on record in the said Court rolls more at large appeareth; now, know ye that we, the said Governor, Treasurer and Assistants, as agents, and in behalf of the said Colony, for and in consideration of the full and just sum of one thousand and one hundred pounds in lawful money of New England, to us in hand, before the ensealing and delivering of these presents, well and truly paid by Edward Gray, of Plymouth, in the Colony aforesaid; Nathaniel Thomas, of Marshfield, in the Colony aforesaid; Benjamin Church, of Puncatest, in the Colony aforesaid; Christopher Almy, Job Almy and Thomas Waite, of Portsmouth, in the Colony of Rhode Island and Providence Plantations; Daniel Wilcox, of Puncatest, and William Manchester, of Puncatest, in the Colony of New Plymouth aforesaid, with which the said sum, we, the said agents, do acknowledge to be fully satisfied, contented and paid, and thereof do acquit and discharge the said [grantees] and their heirs, executors, administrators and assigns forever; by these presents have given, granted, bargained, sold, aliened, enfeoffed and confirmed; and by these presents for us and the said Colony of New Plymouth, do freely, fully and absolutely give, grant, &c., to the said [grantees] all those lands situate, lying and being at Pocasset, and places adjacent in the Colony of Plymouth aforesaid, and is bounded as followeth:—Northward and westward by the Freemen's lot, near the Fall River; westward by the Bay or Sound that runneth between the said lands and Rhode Island; southward partly by Seaconnet bounds, and partly by Dartmouth bounds, and northward and eastward up into the woods till it meets with the lands formerly granted by the Court to other men, and legally obtained by them from the natives, not extending further than Middlebury town bounds and Quitquissit ponds." [Several small reservations previously sold are here named, and the deed proceeds in the usual form, and adds] "that is to say, to the said Edward Gray nine shares or thirtieth parts; to the said Nathaniel Thomas five shares or thirtieth parts; to the said Benjamin Church one share or thirtieth part; to the said Christopher Almy three shares and three-quarters of one share; to the said Job Almy three shares and one-quarter of a share; to the said Thomas Waite one share; to the said Daniel Wilcox two shares; to the said William Manchester five shares." [The rest of the deed is in the usual form of a warrantee deed.]

Signed, sealed and delivered in the presence of witnesses, March 5, 1779-80.

JOSIAH WINSLOW, Governor.
WM. BRADFORD, Treasurer.
THOMAS HINCKLEY, } Assistants.
JAMES CUDWORTH, } Assistants.

Acknowledged March 6, 1679-80.

NOTE E—PAGE 21.

"Nov. 1, 1700. Know all men by these presents, that whereas we, Josiah Winslow, Robert Durfee and Henry Brightman, being chosen agents by the proprietors of Freetown; and Christopher Almy, Samuel Little and Richard Borden, being chosen agents by the proprietors of Tiverton, to run and settle the purchase bounds between the aforesaid Freetown and Tiverton; we have accordingly performed the same as followeth: beginning at a cleft rock on the East side of the country road, near the Fall River, said rock being the bounds of the Freemen's first lot; and from said rock ranging Southwest and by West to the river at the westerly side of the country road, and from thence the river to be the bounds westerly unto Taunton river; and from the aforesaid rock, ranging East Southeast four miles into the woods by a range of marked trees unto a heap of stones with several trees marked about it; and from said heap of stones ranging Northeast and by North one degree northerly by a range of marked trees unto a stone set in the ground, with other stones laid about it, being the head of the four mile line from Stacy's creek; said range to extend till it meet with Middlebury town bounds. These aforementioned boundaries, thus run and settled, we do mutually agree, shall be the perpetual bounds between the land of the aforesaid proprietors of Freetown and the proprietors of Tiverton.

In witness whereof, we, the aforesaid agents have hereunto jointly and severally set our hand the day and year first above written.

Signed and delivered in presence of us. ⎱ JACOB SAMSON, his SAMUEL ⋈ SHERMAN. mark. ⎰	HENRY BRIGHTMAN, ROBERT DURFEE, JOSIAH WINSLOW, RICHARD BORDEN, CHRISTOPHER ALMY, SAMUEL LITTLE.

NOTE F—PAGE 23.

A few words are necessary to explain, what is to be understood by OLD STYLE and NEW STYLE.

The Julian Calendar proceeded on the supposition that a year is 365 days and 6 hours; whereas in truth, an annual revolution of the sun is performed in 365 days, 5 hours, 48 minutes and 45 1-2 seconds; so that the Julian civil year was too long, and exceeded the solar year by 11 minutes and 14 1-2 seconds; which, in about 130 years amounted to one day. Pope Gregory XIII. corrected the error, in 1582. The time, as computed by the Julian method (which is called Old Style,) had then advanced ten days beyond the true time. He ordered that ten days should be suppressed, and that thenceforth three days should be dropped every 400 years, which would be nearly equivalent to one day in 130 years.

The year under the Old Style began the 25th of March: he ordered that it should begin the 1st of January. This new reckoning was called New Style. It was not adopted in England and this country till 1752, when the error had reached eleven days. In old records, deeds and other papers, we find, between 1st of January and 25th of March, double dates, as Jan. 17, 1717–18, which means 1717 Old Style, and 1718 New Style. Another perplexity often arises from not recollecting that January and February were the latter part of the year. For instance, a distinguished man, who died a hundred years ago in February, it was said preached an ordination sermon in July of the same year, which was true, reckoning according to Old Style. Another example: King George III. in May, 1746, ordered Tiverton to be set to Rhode Island, and the Legislature afterwards, in obedience to that order, in January of the same year, incorporated anew the town of Tiverton. The act of incorporation took place the latter end of the year 1746, Old Style, or the beginning of the year 1747, New Style. The practice of double dating between 1st of January and 25th of March, was dropped after 1752.

NOTE G—PAGE 37.

The General School Committee chosen annually by the town of Fall River, and the sums voted to be raised for the support of the Public Schools, are as follows :—

1826—Joseph Hathaway, James Ford, Jason H. Archer, John Lindsey, Wm. B. Canedy. $600 voted.

1827—James Ford, Joseph Hathaway, Jason H. Archer, John Lindsey, Wm. B. Canedy. $1,288 voted.

1828—Thos. M. Smith, Arthur A. Ross, Edward T. Taylor, James Ford, John Eddy. $1,200 voted.

1829—James Ford, Thos. M. Smith, Arthur A. Ross, Hezekiah Battelle, John Eddy. $1,200 voted.

1830—Thos. M. Smith, Jason H. Archer, Arnold Buffum, Foster Hooper, Thomas Wilbur. $1,200 voted.

1831—Foster Hooper, Thos. M. Smith, Thomas Wilbur, Bradley Miner, Leander P. Lovell. $2,000 voted.

1832—Thomas Wilbur, Orin Fowler, Harvey Chace, Bradley Miner, Nathan Durfee. $2,500 voted.

1833—Orin Fowler, Harvey Chace, Nathan Durfee, Thomas Wilbur, Harvey Harnden, James Ford. $3,000 voted.

1834—Orin Fowler, Asa Bronson, Harvey Chace, Philip R. Bennett, Thomas Wilbur, Nathan Durfee. $3,000 voted.

1835—Orin Fowler, Asa Bronson, Simon Clough, George W. Briggs, Nathan Durfee, James Ford. $3,500 voted.

1836—David Anthony, James Ford, Harvey Chace. $3,500 voted.

1837—James Ford, Joseph F. Lindsey, Benjamin B. Sisson, George W. Briggs, Orin Fowler. $4,250 voted.

1838—Joseph F. Lindsey, James Ford, Benjamin B. Sisson, Orin Fowler, Eliab Williams. $4,000 voted.

1839—Orin Fowler, Asa Bronson, James Ford, Eliab Williams, Joseph F. Lindsey. $4,500 voted.

1840—Orin Fowler, Asa Bronson, James Ford, Eliab Williams, Joseph F. Lindsey, Jonathan S. Thompson, George M. Randall. $4,500 voted.

The following persons have held the office of Town Clerk of the town of Fall River :—

Walter D. Chaloner, elected 1803 ; Benjamin Brightman, 1804 ; Wm. B. Canedy, 1814 : Nathaniel Luther, 1816 ; Joseph E. Read, 1817 ; John C. Borden, 1821 ; Nathaniel B. Borden, 1825 ; Benjamin Anthony, 1826 ; Stephen K. Crary, 1831 ; Benjamin Earl, 1836.

The following persons have held the office of Selectmen of Fall River :—

1803—Thomas Borden, Benjamin Durfee, Robert Miller.
1804—Samuel Thurston, Benjamin Durfee, Robert Miller.
1805—Nathan Bowen, Pardon Davol, Elijah Blossom, Jr.
1806—Jonathan Brownell, Abraham Bowen, Elijah Blossom, Jr.
1807—Jonathan Brownell, Elijah Blossom, Stephen Leonard.
1808—Nathan Bowen, Henry Brightman, David Wilson.
1809—David Wilson, William Read, Jr., Charles Durfee.
1810—Charles Durfee, David Wilson, Wm. Read, Jr.
1811—David Wilson, Wm. Read, Jr., Benjamin Bennett, 2d.
1812—Hezekiah Wilson, William B. Canedy, William Borden.
1813—William B. Canedy, William Borden, Isaac Winslow.
1814—William Borden, Benjamin W. Brown, Simmons Hathaway.
1815—Benjamin W. Brown, Sheffel Weaver, Bradford Durfee.
1816—Sheffel Weaver, William Ashley, William Read.
1817—Sheffel Weaver, Abraham Bowen, William Ashley.
1818—'19—Benjamin W. Brown, Charles Pitman, James G. Bowen.
1820—Sheffel Weaver, Benjamin W. Brown, Richard Borden, 2d.
1821-'2—Robert Miller, Charles Pitman, Enoch French.
1823—Joseph E. Read, Benjamin W. Brown, Edmund Chace.
1824-'5-'6-'7—Enoch French, Hezekiah Wilson, William Read.
1828-'9—Enoch French, Sheffel Weaver, William Read.
1830—Sheffel Weaver, John Eddy, William Read.
1831—Samuel Chace, Robinson Buffington, William Ashley.
1832—Samuel Chace, Leonard Garfield, William Ashley.
1833—Samuel Chace, Matthew C. Durfee, Elijah Pierce.
1834—Samuel Chace, Azariah Shove, Smith Winslow.
1835—'6-'7-'8—John Eddy, Israel Anthony, Luther Winslow.
1839—John Eddy, Israel Anthony, Russel Hathaway.
1840—Nathaniel B. Borden, Israel Anthony, William Read.

NOTE H—PAGE 38.

The number of children in the town of Fall, in 1840, between the ages of 4 and 16, is in District No. 1, 291 ; No. 2, 139 ; No. 11, 603 ; No. 12, 400 ; No. 14, 48; total in the village, 1,481. District No. 3, 32; No. 4, 80 ; No. 5, 49; No. 6, 26; No. 7, 18; No. 8, 31; No. 9, 14; No. 10, 13; No. 13, 45; total out of the village, 308. Total in the town, 1,789.

NOTE I—PAGE 38.

Since Fall River was incorporated, in 1803, there have been thirteen regular practising Physicians in this town, namely:

Doct.'s John Turner,* Ashbel Willard,† Amery Glazier, Jason H. Archer, Thomas Wilbur, Nathan Durfee, Foster Hooper, Benjamin B. Sisson†, Thos. T. Wells,† Amos C. Wilbur, William H. A. Crary, Henry Willard.

There have been ten persons practising Law, to wit:

Oakes Anger,* John Lindsey, George B. Holmes,* James Ford, Joseph Hathaway,† Hezekiah Battelle, Cyrus Alden, Eliab Williams, George Paine,* William J. A. Bradford.†

The following persons have held the office of Justice of the Peace:

George Brightman,* James Brightman*, Charles Durfee,* Joseph E. Read, William B. Canedy, Hezekiah Wilson, Cyrus Alden, James Ford, Hezekiah Battelle, Joseph Goodding,† Eliab Williams, Israel Anthony, Benjamin B. Sisson,† Benjamin Anthony,* Joseph Hathaway,† Anthony Mason, David Anthony, Nathaniel B. Borden, John Fessenden.†

Hon. Nathaniel B. Borden, of this town, was a member of the 24th and the 25th Congress; and is the member elect of the 27th Congress of the United States, for District No. 10, Mass.

The following persons, citizens of Fall River, have been members of the Senate of Massachusetts: Hon. Thomas Durfee, from 1781 to 1788; Hon. John Eddy 1838; Hon. Foster Hooper 1840-'41.

The following persons have been Representatives in the General Court of Massachusetts:

1803—Voted not to elect. 104—Abraham Bowen.

1805-'6—Jonathan Brownell. 1807-'8—Abraham Bowen.

1809-'10-'11-'12-'13—Robert Miller.

1814-'15—Joseph E. Read. 1816-'17—Hezekiah Wilson.

1818-'19—Joseph E. Read. 1820—Voted not to elect.

1821—Abraham Bowen. 1822—Robert Miller.

1823-'24—Wm. B. Canedy. 1825—James Ford. 1826—Voted not to elect.

1827—Joseph Hathaway. 1828—Enoch French.

1829—Joseph E. Read, Enoch French, Anthony Mason.

1830—Frederick Winslow, Anthony Mason, Joseph E. Read.

1831—Nathaniel B. Borden, Foster Hooper, Frederick Winslow.

1832—Simeon Borden, Azariah Shove, Anthony Mason, Barnabas Blossom.

1833—Simeon Borden, Azariah Shove, Smith Winslow, Isaac Borden, Earl Chace.

1834—Nath'l B. Borden, Micah H. Ruggles, Anthony Mason, Jervis Shove, William Winslow.

1835—Micah H. Ruggles, Anthony Mason, Philip R. Bennett, Job B. French, Elijah Peirce.

1836—Micah H. Ruggles, Anthony Mason, Caleb B. Vickery, Wm. Ashley, Gilbert H. Durfee.

---

*Deceased. †Removed from town.

J

1837—Micah H. Ruggles, Cyrus Alden, John Eddy, Constant B. Wyatt, Richard C. French, Philip S. Brown.

1838—Frederick Winslow, Benjamin B. Sisson, Philip S. Brown, Hezekiah Battelle.

1539—Micah H. Ruggles, Iram Smith, G. Brightman, 2d, John A. Harris.

1840—John Eddy, Perez Mason, Nathan Durfee, Enoch French.

1841—Nathan Durfee, Job B. French, Lindon Cook.

NOTE K—PAGE 40.

The petition referred to on page 40, is omitted for want of room.

NOTE L—PAGE 44.

The Rev. Silas Brett had eight children, five sons and three daughters, to wit: Olive, born 1749; Joshua Howard, 1751; Susannah, 1753; Thankful, 1755; Silas, 1757; Ebenezer, 1761; Calvin, 1763; Silas, 1767. Joshua Howard Brett was a respectable physician; settled first at Assonet; then in Delaware county, New York, where he died 1822. Calvin, who resides at Easton, is the only one of the above now living.

Seventh Generation.	Eighth Generation.	Ninth Generation.
Children	G. Children	
do	do	
do	do	
do	do	
do	do	
do	do	
do	do	
do		
do		
do		
do		
do		
do		

In Fall River, persons who paid taxes by town, 49—total, 91. Of Read, 42; Freetown, 4—total, 46. Of Brightman, Brightman and Davis families, I have ...ons.

...les, lived and died at Portsmouth, R I. of his nine children settled at Fall River; ...m are scattered over the United States, only children, whose descendants have

...of Fall River. Joseph was killed in a ...e of Fall River. Stephen, of the third ...n Abraham, who was the father of the ...the ancestor, in the Borden line, of all

...h ...tion.	Sixt Genera
	Joseph
	Phebe
	William
	Isaac
	Thomas
...ce ...s	Sally
	Hope
	Irene
	Richard
	Mary
	John
	Jefferso
	Maritta
	Abraha
	Amey
	Thomas
	Hannah
	Richard
l	Cook
	Lodowi
	Zephan
	& 2 oth
	Simeon
	Nath'l
......	Ann
	Judith
	Sarah

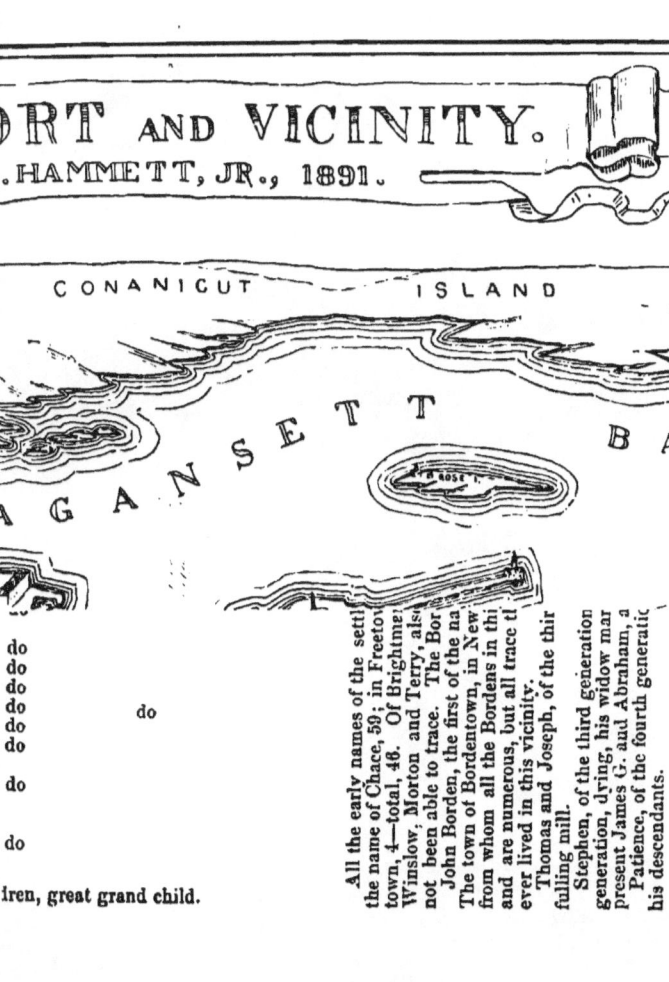

PORT AND VICINITY. HAMMETT, JR., 1891.

CONANICUT ISLAND

...AGANSETT B...

All the early names of the settl... the name of Chace, 52; in Freetou... town, 4—total, 46. Of Brightma... Winslow, Morton and Terry, also ... not been able to trace. The Bor... John Borden, the first of the na... The town of Bordentown, in New ... from whom all the Bordens in thi... and are numerous, but all trace t... ever lived in this vicinity.

Thomas and Joseph, of the thir... fulling mill.

Stephen, of the third generation ...generation, dying, his widow mar ...present James G. and Abraham, a ...Patience, of the fourth generatio... his descendants.

...eph and hers ters.	{ Childre
	Childre
	Mrs Tu
...in	Childre:
...l	Childre
...l	Childre
...e	do
...l	do
	do
...l	do
	do
......	{ Holder } sisters
...l	
...& ...rs	Childrei
	do
...th	
	do
	do
	do
	do
	do
...m	do
...l	do

do		
do		
do		
do	do	
do		
do		
do		
do		

iren, great grand child.

isters, children,

First Generation.	Second Generation.	Third Generation.	Fourth Generation.	Fifth Generation.	Sixth Generation.	Seventh Generation.	Eighth Generation.	Ninth Generation.
					Joseph	Children	G. Children	
					Phebe	do	do	
					William	do	do	
					Isaac	do	do	
					Thomas	do	do	
				Patience	Sally	do	do	
				Thomas	Hope	do		
		Richard......		Sarah	Irene			
				Hope	Richard			
				Betsey	Mary			
	John	Christopher			John			
			Mary	Mary	Jefferson			
		Rebecca			Maritta			
	Thomas...				Abraham			
					Amey			
Richard...			Richard		Thomas			
		Mary			Hannah			
					Richard			
					Cook			
					Lodowick			
					Zephaniah			
					& 2 others			
		Abraham......	Simeon......		Simeon			
John	Joseph ..		Perry		Nath'l D	do	do	
		Samuel	Judith		Ann	do		
	Samuel				Judith	do		
					Sarah	do		
Thomas	Sarah		Col. Joseph					
	Mary	Patience	Durfee, and	Children	Grand	Great grand	Great Great
		Peace	his brothers		Children	Children	Grand
	Rebecca		and sisters.				Children
			Daniel	Children	do	do	
			John	Mrs Turner	do	do	
			Benjamin	Children	do	do	
			Thomas				
William			Sarah	Children	do	do	
		Stephen......	Stephen				
			Nathan	Children	do	do	
			Patience	do	do	do	
Benjamin			Hannah	do	do		
			Lucy	do	do	do	
			Meribah	do	do	do	
Hope	Stephen...		Mary	do	do		
			Lydia				
			Isaiah				
		George......	Sylvia	Mehler &	Children		
Mary		Mary	George...	sisters			
		Hannah	Stephen				
		Penelope	Thomas &				
Joseph		Lusannah	11 others				
		Sarah	Aaron	Children	Gr'd Child	do	
		Joseph	Susan	do	do		
	William ..	William*	Elizabeth				
Amie		Benjamin	Joseph	do	do		
		Parker	Parker	do	do		
		Thomas	Abel	do	do	do	
	George	Stephen	Abner	do	do		
		George	Abby	do	do		
		Ruth	Peace	do	do		
		Ann	Abraham				
		Gideon	Rhoda	do	do		
	Joseph	Rev. Job	Israel				
			David				
			William	do	do		

GENEALOGY OF THE FAMILY OF JOHN BORDEN

* Ruth Durfee and six sisters, children, grand children, great grand child.

All the early names of the settlers of Freetown, continue here. Some of them are numerous. In 1840 there were in Fall River, persons who paid taxes by the name of Chace, 59; in Freetown 12—total, 71. Of Borden, 58; Freetown, 1—total, 59. Of Hathaway, 42; Freetown, 43—total, 85. Of Davis, 57; Freetown, 1—total, 58. Of Durfee, 20; Freetown, 1—total, 29. Of the name of Cudworth, Winslow, able to trace. The genealogy of the Hathaways, and the Durfee family for eight generations, I have been able to trace. The Borden family I have traced for nine generations, and (as is believed,) the father of all of the names in the United States settled at Fall River. Only two of his nine children settled over the United States. John Borden, the first of the name in this region, and (as is believed,) lived and died at Portsmouth, R. I. The town of Bordentown, in New Jersey, it is said, took its name from it. The descendants of the other seven children are scattered over the United States, and are numerous, but all trace their origin to a common source. Richard and Joseph, sons of John Borden, were his only children, whose descendants have ever lived in this vicinity. Richard and Joseph, of the third generation, sons of Richard, inherited the lands and water power on the South side of Fall River. Joseph was killed in a freshet-mill. Thomas and Joseph, of the third generation, (son of Joseph of the second) inherited the lands and water power on the North side of Fall River. Stephen, of the third generation, dying, his widow married John Borden, by whom she had two sons, Nathan and John. Nathan had a son Abraham, who was the father of the present James G. and Abraham, and their sisters. Patience, of the fourth generation, daughter of Joseph, (that was killed) married Hon. Thomas Durfee, and was thus the ancestor, in the Borden line, of all his descendants.

Jeneration.	Fifth Gen.	Sixth Gen.	Seventh Gen.	Eighth Gen.
September, 1748,	Children.	Grand Child.		
ril, 1750,	do.	do.	Great Grand	Great Great
)ril, 1752,			Children.	Grand Ch'n.
May, 1754,	do.	do.	do.	
September, 1756,	do.	do.	do.	
igust, 1759,				
)vember, 1761.	do.	dd.	do.	
November, 1764,	do.			
66,	do.	do.		
3,	do.	do.		
innary, 1771,				
igust, 1773,	do.	do.		
:hard,	do.	do.	do.	
	do.	do.		

.cestor of most who bear his name in this vicinity, lived and died at
iverton, of William Manchester, one of the eight original proprietors, for
spot where Dea. Richard Durfee, his grandson, now resides. Benjamin
3, aged 52. Hon. Thomas Durfee, son of Benjamin, was much in public
:n years; and of the House of Representatives twenty years; in all thirty
usetts. He died July, 1796, aged 75. His wife Patience, (who was the
2, aged 71.
vas of another family, and his descendants, it is said, removed to Mid-

MASSACHUSETTS AND RHODE ISLAND

Boundary Question.

After a controversy between Massachusetts and Rhode Island of almost two hundred years' duration, the Supreme Court of the United States has made a final decision in regard to the respective boundaries of the two States. As the citizens of Fall River have been particularly interested in this subject, from their connection with it in 1846, and as the decision of the Court will very materially influence the future of our city, it is proposed to give a short, concise account of the leading events in the history of this controversy,—more particularly of such as had reference to places in or near Fall River.

In November, 1620, two months subsequent to the sailing of the Mayflower, James, I., King of England, by a charter generally called the Great Patent or Charter of New England, granted to the Plymouth Company, or the Council at Plymouth, in England, the government of a tract of country in America, included between the 40th and the 48th degree of North latitude, and between the Atlantic and "Western" Oceans ; this tract to be called New England.

Our Pilgrim fathers, the pioneers in the settlement of the country thus chartered, formed their own compact of self-government in November, one month before landing at Plymouth, and they continued to act under this compact, with no legal right to the country in which they governed, until 1629, when the Council at Plymouth (Eng.) granted a charter to William Bradford and his associates, in which the boundaries of that part of New England subsequently known as Plymouth Colony, were defined. One-half of the waters mentioned as the Narragansett River, formed her Western limit.*

---

*All the territory included in this charter was purchased of the Indians by the Colonists. The Mount Hope country, (now Bristol,) afterwards confirmed to the Colony by Charles II., was conquered from Philip in 1667.

GENEALOGY OF THE FAMILY OF THOMAS DURFEE,	Benjamin..	James, born Aug. 28, 1701, Ann, January 11, 1705, Hope, January 7, 1703, William, Dec. 3, 1707, Benjamin, Jan. 3, 1709, Mary, Jan. 30, 1711, Lusannah, Jan. 24, 1713, Martha, July 15, 1719, Hon. Thomas, Nov. 9, 1721,	Hope, born September, 1748, Joseph, April, 1750, Nathan, April, 1752, Benjamin, May, 1754, Prudence, September, 1756, Abigail, August, 1759, Charles, November, 1761, Lusannah, November, 1764, Nathan, 1760, James, 1764, Thomas, January, 1771, Samuel, August, 1773,	Children. do. do. do. do. do. do. do.	Grand Child. do. do. do. do. do.	Great Grand Children. do. do. do.	Great Great Grand Ch'n.
		Richard, Nov. 9, 1723,	Ephraim, Sarah, Deacon Richard, Rebecca,	do. do.	do. do.	do.	

Thomas Durfee, the first of the name in this region, and, (as is believed,) the ancestor of most who bear his name in this vicinity, lived and died at Portsmouth, Rhode Island. He purchased, in 1690, one-sixtieth of the town of Tiverton, of William Manchester, one of the eight original proprietors, for £31. This land he gave to his son Benjamin, in 1712, who then resided near the spot where Dea. Richard Durfee, his grandson, now resides. Benjamin Durfee died January 6, 1754, aged 74. His wife Prudence died March 11, 1773, aged 52. Hon. Thomas Durfee, son of Benjamin, was much in public life. He was a member of the Governor's Council three years; of the Senate seven years; and of the House of Representatives twenty years; in all thirty years a member of the Council, or of one branch of the Legislature of Massachusetts. He died July, 1790, aged 73. His wife Patience, (who was the fourth generation from John Borden,) was born August, 1751, and died July, 1812, aged 71.

In the early records of Freetown, Robert Durfee is repeatedly mentioned. He was of another family, and his descendants, it is said, removed to Middleborough.

No proof can be obtained of the confirmation of this charter by the Crown, but the Colonists were recognized as a government by the Kings of England, and continued to hold and exercise jurisdiction over the territory mentioned, for more than one hundred and sixteen years.

In 1643, the Earl of Warwick, and others, granted to Roger Williams the first charter of Rhode Island. This charter did not conflict with the claims of Plymouth; but in 1663, Charles II. granted another patent to the citizens of Rhode Island, by which some parts of the eastern boundary of that Colony were extended three miles to the east and northeast of Narragansett Bay; all of which territory was claimed by Plymouth.

Plymouth immediately took measures to secure her rights, by application to King Charles, who accordingly appointed commissioners in 1664. These commissioners reported in favor of Plymouth, and their decision was confirmed by the King. From this time until 1746, the disputed territory was governed in accordance with this decision—Plymouth Colony exercising jurisdiction over the tract granted in her first patent, until 1691, when, by a charter from William and Mary, it was united with other territories, to form the Province of Massachusetts. The boundaries remained unchanged, and for the following fifty-five years it was under the government of Massachusetts. Thus for one hundred and sixteen years the boundary of Plymouth, as established by her original charter in 1629, was recognized and confirmed as the true boundary between Massachusetts and Rhode Island.

In 1740, however, Rhode Island again applied to the Crown for a re-examination of her eastern boundary. She could have had no other encouragement to hope for a successful result of such an application, than the known disposition of England to contract, as much as possible, both the territorial and civil rights of Massachusetts,—a disposition which had just been shown in the settlement of the boundary between that province and New Hampshire. As this settlement gave to New Hampshire more territory than she claimed, Rhode Island had reason for expecting that she too would obtain some advantage by again agitating this question.

In response to the application of Rhode Island, George II. appointed fifteen commissioners, eight of whom met at Providence in 1740, and there examined the claims of both parties. After a session of nearly three months, they made their award, which, although favorable to Rhode Island, was appealed from by both Provinces. This award, nevertheless, was confirmed by the King in 1746. By this decision Little Compton, Tiverton, Bristol, Barrington, Warren and Cumberland, were added to the territory of Rhode Island. For marking the boundaries thus decided upon, commissioners were to be appointed by Rhode Island and Massachusetts, with instructions to run six straight lines (each extending three miles into the territory formerly claimed by Massachusetts;) from points mentioned on Providence River and Narragansett Bay ; the terminations of these six lines to be united by other straight lines, which would form the required boundary.

When this business came before the next session of the Massachusetts legislature, it was found that Rhode Island had already appointed commissioners, who, without waiting for the action of Massachusetts, had run the lines, *ex parte*. Massachusetts (supposing that they had, as they professed to have done, marked the boundary in accordance with the decision of the King,) took no measures for having it examined until 1791, when, in consequence of renewed difficulties, she appointed commissioners, who were empowered to ascertain, run and mark (in conjunction with similarly appointed commissioners from Rhode Island,) the boundary between the two States, in accordance with the directions of the King in 1746, *if such directions could be mutually understood.*

These commissioners proceeded to measure the lines previously run by the *ex parte* commissioners of Rhode Island, and found that in every case they infringed upon the territory of Massachusetts, from eight to one hundred and sixty-eight rods. There was also a disagreement between them as to the proper point of commencing the measurement of that line which forms the southern boundary of Fall River. They could come to no decision in regard to a part of the boundary, and reported thus to their respective legislatures.

Again in 1844, six commissioners (three from each State) were appointed by Massachusetts and Rhode Island, and authorized to establish the true boundary line from the Atlantic Ocean to Burnt Swamp Corner. Two of the Massachusetts commissioners and the three from Rhode Island came to the same conclusion as to the proper line, and their report, with that of the minority, was presented to the legislature on the 13th of January, 1848. When matters had proceeded thus far, and the question which had been agitated for two hundred years was apparently about to be settled, its decision was again delayed.

At this time the townsmen of Fall River appointed Orin Fowler, Foster Hooper and Phineas W. Leland, a committee to petition the Massachusetts legislature not to allow any settlement of the boundary less advantageous than that granted by George II. in 1741. The question in which Fall River felt particularly interested, was in regard to the proper position of one of the three mile lines, which, as run by the *ex parte* commissioners of Rhode Island, passed through the town, but which it was now claimed should have been run farther to the south. The facts in the matter were as follows :—In their award of 1741, the King's commissioners gave special directions in regard to the points from which measurements were to be made in finding and marking the true boundary. These directions all subsequent commissioners professed to follow ; but the petitioners of Fall River claimed that they had not done so in respect (among other points) to one mentioned in the King's award as "a certain point four hundred and forty rods to the southward of the mouth of Fall River," from which a line was to be run three miles toward the east, forming the northern boundary of that part of Rhode Island.

In measuring this 440 rods, the *ex parte* commissioners of 1746 "measured round a cove or inlet, and followed the sinuosities of the shore " until they reached a point from a quarter to a half mile farther north than if the same distance had been measured in a straight line. From this point they extended the three mile line, running it through the village of Fall River, and the boundary thus established had since remained unchanged.

The Fall River petitioners claimed, and gave reason for such claim, that George II., in his decision of 1746, designed that the point from which to run the three mile line should be 440 rods in a *direct* line from the mouth of the Fall River. They showed that in making these measurements as they had, the Rhode Island commissioners added to their State a thickly settled territory, with about fifteen hundred inhabitants, and a taxable property valued at nearly half a million of dollars ; when, if the measurements had been made in straight lines, not only would the designs of George II. and his commissioners have been carried out, but Fall River would have been brought within the bounds of one State, with no danger of its thickly settled territory being again placed under a divided jurisdiction.

In consequence of facts and arguments presented by the Fall River petitioners, the Massachusetts legislature refused to ratify the decision of their commissioners. Soon after, in 1852, the two States filed bills of equity, thus transferring the question under dispute to the Supreme Court, agreeing to conform to whatever decision it should arrive at.

In 1860 the Supreme Court appointed engineers, with instructions to measure and mark a described line. This line in 1861 was established by the decree of that Court, as the true boundary between the two States, this decree to take effect in March, 1862. In its decision, the Court granted the full claim of neither State. Not professing to run the line in accordance with the decision of the King's commissioners of 1741, it placed it so as to give, as far as possible, an undivided jurisdiction to densely populated districts—as Fall River and Pawtucket,—without infringing upon the rights of either party.

The boundary, as marked, passes between Fall River and Tiverton, and so far as respects the present boundary of the City of Fall River, is described as "crossing Mount Hope Bay to the westerly end of the line dividing Fall River and Tiverton, where the same intersects low water line of said Mount Hope Bay. Thence easterly, following said dividing line between Fall River and Tiverton, passing through the middle of a town way on the north side of a farm belonging to John Chase, and through the southerly end of Cook Pond to a line passing through the middle of a highway eight rods wide. Thence running southerly through the centre of said eight rod highway, to a point in line with the stone wall on the northerly side of the farm of Edmund Estes. This wall is easterly of the Stafford road, so called. Thence running easterly in line with said wall to a point in line of highest water mark on the westerly shore of South Watuppa Pond. Thence southerly by line of highest water mark of said Watuppa Pond and of Sawdy Pond and of the streams connecting them to the most southerly end of Sawdy Pond, where it meets the line of the westerly side of the Town of Westport.

By this change of boundary, Massachusetts acquires a territory the area of which is about eleven square miles. Of this about nine square miles, with a population of 3,593, and a taxable property of $1,948,378, are embraced within the limits of the City of Fall River.

THE GREAT FIRE OF 1843.

Sunday, July 2d, •1843, will always be referred to by the inhabitants of this city, as a day on which occured one of the most memorable events recorded in the history of Fall River.   It furnishes a date from which incidents are often reckoned, and "before the fire" and "after the fire" are terms well understood and in common use among the people.   The direct influence and effect of that event are seen and felt at the present time.   The fire-bell never strikes without awakening a remembrance of the disastrous results which once followed such an alarm ; and whether at mid-day or mid-night, the alarm is scarcely sounded before our firemen are at their posts, our steam and hand engines in working order, and our streets filled with anxious and interested "lookers on."   All this gives to our citizens a feeling of security which they could not have felt on that Sabbath afternoon when they were called from their places of worship to arrest a great conflagration with a comparatively inefficient fire department.

During a part of the day on which the fire occurred, the mercury stood at 90°.   Every thing was dry and parched, after a long drought ; the water was shut off from the stream, that labor might be performed in its channel ; and a high wind was blowing from the southwest, tending greatly to facilitate the progress of the flames. The alarm of fire was given at about 4 o'clock P. M.   The conflagration commenced near the corner of Main and Borden streets, in an open space in the rear of a large three-story warehouse occupied by Abner L. Westgate.   This space was covered with shavings, which were kindled from the firing of a small cannon by two boys. The fire almost instantly communicated with the surrounding buildings, and within five minutes the flames were rising apparently fifty feet high.   Showers of sparks and cinders, carried by the heavy wind, kindled many buildings before they were reached by the body of the fire.

The buildings on both sides of Main Street were soon burning, and the wind blowing nearly parallel with the street, all hope of controlling the flames and saving the business part of the village, was abandoned. So sudden were the movements of the flames, unexpectedly rising in different localities, that in many cases all efforts to preserve property were ineffectual.

The whole space between Main, Franklin, Rock and Borden streets was one vast sheet of fire, entirely beyond the control of man ; and had not the foe proved the ally, the destruction would have continued until nearly the whole village was in ruins. The change in the direction of the wind was all that checked the flames.

Man was powerless, and could only helplessly and with fear view the terrible scene. Awe as well as terror must have influenced the beholders, when to the crackling flames, the crash of falling timber, and the whistling of the wind, were added the lightning's flash and the thunder's deep roar. They looked upon their village in ruins, and felt that it must long bear the marks of this fearful calamity. They could not foresee that so terrible a catastrophe would warm into new life the industrial activities of the place, and that in eleven years Fall River would be numbered among the cities of the Commonwealth. They did not dream that in ten years its population would be increased two-thirds, and its taxable property doubled ; and that in twenty years, instead of running but thirty-two thousand spindles in its representative business, almost two hundred thousand would be employed in manufacturing forty-five millions of yards of cloth.

While Dr. Archer's house, on the southeast corner of Main and Franklin streets, was burning, the wind, which had been blowing from the southwest, suddenly changed to the northward, driving back the flames over the burnt district. The house of H. Battelle, Esq., on Purchase street, was the last building burned, and the only one north of Franklin street. It took fire at about ten o'clock P. M. While it was in flames, a vessel arrived at the wharf with an engine company from Bristol. The company immediately proceeded to Purchase street, and by their timely efforts saved the adjoining buildings and prevented the further progress of the flames.

The conflagration had swept over nearly twenty acres of the central part of the village. After immediate danger was passed, the remaining dwellings were thrown open, and shelter and refreshment

K

furnished to many houseless and exhausted people ; but a great number passed the night in the open air.

Soon after the fire, a committee was appointed, with instructions to obtain a correct list of those who had suffered, and of the amount of property destroyed. From the report published by this committee, it appears that the

" No. of persons residing within the burnt district at
    the time of the fire, was.................. 1,324
No. of persons in addition, employed or doing busi-
    ness in the burnt district, but living out, about   600
Buildings burned,............................ 291
Hotels,..................................... 2
Churches, ... 3
Cotton Factory,............................. 1
Carriage Factories,....,.................... 2
Banks,..................................... 2
Cabinet Warehouses,........................ 3
Marble Factory,............................. 1
Tannery,................................... 1
Livery Stables,............................. 4
Dry Goods Establishments,.................. 17
Clothing   " 11
Grocery and Provision Establishments, including
    three or four Crockery Stores connected,..... 24
Boot and Shoe Stores,...................... 6
Hat and Cap   " 3
Book and Periodical Stores,................. 3
Hardware,.................................. 3
Millinery Shops,............................ 11
Mantua Makers,............................ 5
Apothecaries, ... 6
Jewelers,.................................. 3
Harness Makers,........................... 3
Stove and Tinware,......................... 3
Brass Founderies,.......................... 2
Blacksmith Shops,.......................... 3
Machine   " 2
Carpenters'   " 8
Reed Makers' " 1

Shoe Makers' Shops,........................ 7
Plane Makers' Shop,....................... 1
Roll Covers   "   ....;...,.... 1
Turners,.................................. 1
Paint Shops,.............................. 8
Butchers' Shops,.......................... 4
Soap Boiler Shop,......................... 1
Cigar Factory,..........................,. 1
Restaurateurs,............................ 7
Bake Houses,.............................. 2
School House,............................. 1
School Rooms, beside,..................... 3
- Athenæum,................................ 1
Custom House,............................. 1
Post Office,.............................. 1
Auction Room,............................. 1
Counting Rooms,........................... 7
Dentists' Offices,........................ 2
Stage Office,............................. 1
Printing Offices,......................... 3
Lawyers'   " 5
Physicians' " 5
Barbers' Shops,........................... 3

" Whole Amount of Loss on Buildings,...... $264,470
  "   "   "   Other Property,... 262,015

    Total Loss on both,................ $526,485

Total Insurance on Buildings,.............. $102,955
  "   "   Other Property,.......... 74,020

    Whole Amount of Insurance,......... $176,975

    Excess of Loss over Insurance,....... $349,510"

The day after the fire, a committee was appointed by the citizens
to afford relief to those who had suffered. This committee entered
immediately upon their duties, and presented a circular which called
forth so much sympathy and was so liberally responded to, that we
quote it entire.

NOTE.—All the merchandize shops in the place were destroyed, except some six
or eight, (principally groceries) situated in the extreme parts of the village."

CIRCULAR.

"To their fellow-citizens, near and remote, both in town and country, the undersigned, a Committee in behalf of the people of Fall River, Mass., make this their brief appeal for help, amid the appalling calamity which, under the wise and righteous Providence of God, has overtaken us.

Our population, from 8,000 to 9,000 souls, and chiefly devoted to manufacturing and mechanic pursuits, is in deep distress—a portion of it in pressing want.

At 4 o'clock P. M., last Sabbath, the 2d inst., a fire broke out in a central part of this village, (the wind blowing a gale) which in its ravages was of the most desolating character.

The burnt district comprises some fifteen or twenty acres of the centre of business operations.

Nearly 200 buildings (not including many small ones) are consumed; among which are three newly built houses of public worship, and all our public offices. Our post office and custom house are gone, and we have not a printing office, nor hotel, nor bank building, nor book store, nor market, nor bakery left. Nearly all our grocery and provision stores, including one wholesale establishment, with most of their contents; and all our dry goods, druggist, tailor, milliner, tin ware, and paint shops, with one cotton factory, running 3,000 spindles, are gone.

Nearly 200 families are turned houseless, and many of them pennyless into the street.

Besides, this appalling fire raged with such fury, and spread with such velocity, that many of the sufferers gladly escaped with their lives, without a pillow for their heads, or a change of raiment for their backs. The amount of property consumed it is impossible to estimate, even by anything like a probable approximation.

The assessors of the town, in the discharge of their official duties, within the last two months, have rated the property of the place at three and a half millions of dollars—and the heart of the village is in ashes.

We cannot, we need not enlarge.

We tell you in few words the simple, sad story of our calamity; and with the scene of desolation before us, and the cries of distress around us, we ask your aid:—In behalf of our suffering neighbors, and in the name of humanity, and of our Heavenly Father, we appeal to your kindness and your love, and solicit your assistance ; not to repair our losses and rebuild our village, but to relieve our present distress, and enable us to give bread to the hungry, clothing to the naked, and shelter to the houseless ; until, with due effort on the part of all among us, a merciful and righteous God, who has justly afflicted us, shall command the hum of business, the smile of contentment and the song of joy to return to our now desolate borders. Send us what you can send—food, clothing, money—send it addressed to either of us, and it shall be carefully distributed to the needy.

N. B.—Provisions or other articles by the way of Providence, Rhode Island, may be sent to the care of Capt. Thomas Borden, of the steamboat King Philip, which plies daily between that port and ours.

JERVIS SHOVE,	DAVID ANTHONY,
ORIN FOWLER,	ASA BRONSON,
JOHN EDDY,	RICHARD BORDEN,
JEFFERSON BORDEN,	WILLIAM BROWN,
ENOCH FRENCH,	JOSEPH F. LINDSEY,
	Committee.

Fall River, Mass., July 4th, 1843.

Prompt and generous donations of money, clothing and food were received in quantities sufficient to prevent immediate suffering.

From Boston, were received	$13,165 00
" Providence,	1,700 00
" New Bedford,	1,700 00
" Cambridge,	1,000 00
" One church in Charlestown,	650 00
" Pawtucket and vicinity,	637 00
" The churches in Newburyport,	600 00
" David S. Brown & Co., Philadelphia	250 00
" Bristol,	208 00
" Dorchester,	106 00
" Tiffany Ward & Co., Baltimore,	100 00

The whole amount of money received by the committee was $50.934 00.

ECCLESIASTICAL STATISTICS.*

THE FIRST BAPTIST CHURCH

Of Fall River was organized in 1781. The names of pastors who have officiated since 1840, are as follows :—Rev. Asa Bronson until 1846. Rev. Velona R. Hotchkiss, D. D., from 1846 to 1850. Rev. A. P. Mason, D. D., from 1850 to 1853. Rev. J. R. Scott from 1853 to 1854 ; and Rev. P. B. Haughwout, the present pastor, since 1855. The number of communicants connected with the Church in 1861, was 323. Number of pupils connected with Sabbath School, 275 ; average attendance of pupils, 176.

In this connection, mention should be made of the second pastor of the Church, Rev. Job. Borden. One of his successors has furnished the following sketch :

REV. JOB BORDEN.

Among that noble band of Baptist ministers, hard-handed and stout-hearted, to whom the cause of evangelical religion, and in particular, the Baptist representation of that cause, in this part of the Commonwealth of Massachusetts, are so largely indebted, the venerable Job Borden holds an honorable and eminent place.

He was a man of vigorous intellect ; unusually clear in his perceptions, and firm in his convictions ; yet void of narrow-mindedness, and possessed of a generous and catholic spirit ; a man worthy to be classed with those whose earnest faith and self-denying labors have won, from the gratitude and affection of the church, the title of " Fathers in Israel."

In his early manhood, and before he assumed the office of a christian minister, he was afflicted with the total loss of his eye-sight. And thenceforward, through his long and unusually active life, in all that he accomplished, his efforts were subject to the painful drawback and hindrance of this grievous calamity. Deprived of those advan-

---

*For statistics previous to 1840, see pp. 45–56.

tages which our schools and colleges confer ; shut out, by his blindness, from the ordinary sources of knowledge, save as they were opened to him by the kindness of those around him; compelled by his circumstances to depend mainly upon the labor of his own hands for the support of his family ; required, by the exigencies of the time, and the feeble and widely scattered membership of the church, to travel from place to place, and visit from house to house, preaching at all seasons and as opportunities arose ; it is surprising to us that he contrived, in the face of so many obstacles, and under such discouraging embarrassments, to acquire a knowledge of the Scriptures, and a readiness and expertness in the use of it, which were deemed remarkable by his cotemporaries, and which, together with the natural force and quickness of his mind, called forth the homely but honest encomium of the historian Bacchus :—" He is blind, indeed, as to natural sight, but he hath such spiritual light as to be esteemed a clear preacher of the gospel."

There are are some among us who still recall the figure of this devoted and laborious servant of Christ, as he went about in his later years, riding upon his old white horse, which, like John Wesley's famous itinerant, had learned to travel, with unerring sagacity, all the rounds of his master.

Father Borden was the first pastor of the Baptist church in Freetown, and continued in that office for forty-two years. And although his decaying strength, and the weight of his many years, made it necessary that the church should summon the aid of other and younger pastors, yet nothing was done to break or impair his tenure of office ; and he remained as a Pastor Emeritus, and prolonged the labors of his earlier.years until God called him to his reward. He was twice married, and his widow, who was a school-teacher at the time of her marriage, and who seems to have devoted herself to her husband, and labored to compensate for his great misfortune, in an unusual degree, is still living, in a green old age, among the children of those who listened with her to the sound doctrine and persuasive counsel of her husband.*

---

*A very good portrait of Father Borden, the generous gift of his widow, hangs upon the walls of the Committee-room, in the First Baptist Church. The remains of father Borden, with those of his first wife, repose in a small grave-yard near the "Narrows," on the site of the first house of worship erected by the church.

THE FIRST CONGREGATIONAL CHURCH

Was organized January 9, 1816. The names of those who have been pastors subsequent to 1840, are, Rev. Orin Fowler, dismissed in May, 1850. Rev. Benjamin Relyea, installed in May, 1850, dismissed in April, 1856. Rev. J. Lewis Diman, ordained in December, 1856, dismissed in February, 1860. Rev. Solomon P. Fay, the present pastor, installed in May, 1861. The membership of the church in 1861, was 204. Number of pupils connected with the Sabbath School, 250. Average attendance of pupils, 150.

A SOCIETY OF FRIENDS

Was organized about the year 1817. In 1844, a division took place among the members. A part removed to their meeting house on Franklin street, and the others continued to worship in their building on Main street. The former have no regularly appointed minister. In 1861, they numbered 70 members. The Society which worships on Main street, had in 1861, 115 members. The number of scholars connected with their Sabbath School is 45 ; average attendance, 32.

THE FIRST METHODIST EPISCOPAL CHURCH

Was organized in June, 1827. The names of pastors who have officiated since 1840 are given, with date of their ordination :— 1840, Rev. Isaac Bonney ; 1842, Rev. Thomas Ely ; 1844, Rev. George F. Pool ; 1845, Rev. James D. Butler ; 1847, Rev. David Patten ; 1849, Rev. Daniel Wise ; 1851, Rev. Frederic Upham ; 1853, Rev. Elisha B. Bradford ; 1855, Rev. John Howson ; 1857, Rev. Thomas Ely ; 1859, Rev. Andrew McKeown ; 1861, Rev. Chas. H. Payne, the present pastor. The membership of the church in 1861, was 252. Number of pupils connected with Sabbath School, 450 ; average attendance, 280.

THE FIRST CHRISTIAN CHURCH

Was organized in the year 1829. The names of pastors who have been installed since 1840, are : Rev. P. R. Russell, installed January, 1841. Rev. A. M. Averill, March, 1843. Rev. Elijah Shaw, March, 1845. Rev. Charles Morgridge, April, 1847. Rev. Stephen

Fellows, June, 1848. Rev. David E. Millard supplied the pulpit
six months. Rev. B. S. Fanton, January, 1853. Rev. Warren
Hathaway, installed March, 1855; dismissed October, 1860. There
has been no settled pastor since 1860. The membership of the
Church in 1861, was 280. Increase of membership since 1840,
259. Number of scholars connected with Sabbath School, 215 ;
average attendance, 151.

THE FIRST UNITARIAN CHURCH

Was organized in 1832. The names of pastors who have been ordained since 1840, are : Rev. John F. W. Ware, ordained in May,
1843. Rev. Samuel Longfellow, in February, 1848. Rev. Josiah
K. Waite, in September, 1852. Rev. W. B. Smith, the present
pastor, January, 1860. The number of communicants connected
with the Church in 1861, was 50. The number of families connected with the Society is 126. Number of pupils connected with
Sabbath School is 173; average attendance, 110. In 1860, the
church located on Second street was taken down, and a portion of
the old materials used in the erection of the present house of worship, on North Main street.

THE CHURCH OF THE ASCENSION

Was organized in 1836. The Rev. George M. Randall entered upon
his duties as pastor, July, 1838, but was not installed rector until
1840. The Rev. Amos D. McCoy succeeded him in 1845, and remained a little over two years. In 1849, the present incumbent,
Rev. E. M. Porter, entered upon his duties as rector. The number
of communicants connected with the Church in 1861, was 112.
Number of Scholars connected with Sabbath School, about 300 ;
average attendance, 208.

In 1850, the Society suffered a severe loss in the destruction of its
church edifice by fire; but after more than a year of exertions on
the part of the parish, and with assistance from abroad, they were
enabled to erect the small but tasteful structure in which they now
worship.

SAINT MARY'S CHURCH,
(*Roman Catholic*,)

Was established in 1836. The first name was St. John Baptist,
which was changed upon the occupation of their new cathedral in

L

1855. The corner stone of this cathedral was laid by the Right Rev. Fitzpatric, Bishop of Boston, August 8, 1852. The dimensions of the structure are 67 feet by 150. It is built in the Gothic style, and of uncut granite. The first pastor of the church was Rev. John Corry ; second pastor, Rev. Richard Hardy ; third pastor, the present incumbent, Rev. E. Murphy, appointed April, 1840.

THE CENTRAL CHURCH,

(*Congregational,*)

Was organized November 16, 1843. Rev. Samuel Washburn, the first pastor, was installed April 24, 1844, and dismissed January 2, 1849. Rev. Eli Thurston, the present pastor, was installed March 21, 1849. The whole number received into the church since its organization is 396, of whom 195 were received upon profession. There have been dismissed to other churches 96, 52 have died, a number have been excommunicated, leaving 232 as the present membership. The number of scholars in the Sabbath School is 260. Average attendance 173.

THE SECOND BAPTIST CHURCH,

Worshipping in the Baptist Temple on South Main street, was organized in June, 1846 by 157 persons, mostly from the First Baptist Church in this city. Rev. Asa Bronson was the first pastor, and remained in this office until October, 1857.

Revivals of religion have signally marked the history of this church. The aggregate increase during the fifteen years of its history has been 433, of which about 300 have been by baptism. The decrease in the same period has been 281. The present number is 309. The Sabbath School numbers 350, with an average attendance, the past year, of 245.

Rev. Charles Snow, the present pastor of this church, was ordained and installed July 7, 1858.

THE UNITED PRESBYTERIAN CHURCH

Was organized in 1846. The number of members at that time was 22. For five years after the organization there was no stated pastor, and only occasional religious service. The first pastor, Rev. David A. Wallace, was installed June, 1851 ; the second, and present pastor, Rev. William Maclaren, in November, 1854.

According to the last annual report, dated May, 1861, the number of church members was 140, and the number of families, 110. The whole congregation numbers about 400. The number of scholars connected with the Sabbath School is 150.

The place of worship on Pearl street was purchased by the Society in 1849. Aided efficiently by the influence and efforts of their present pastor, they completed the payment of the church debt in June, 1861, and they now own their commodious and substantial church edifice and the ground connected with it, free of all incumbrance.

ST. PAUL'S METHODIST EPISCOPAL CHURCH

Was organized April 20, 1851. The names of its pastors since that time, with date of their installation, are:—1851, Rev. Daniel Wise ; 1853, Rev. John Hobart ; 1855, Rev. M. J. Talbot ; 1857, Rev. Samuel C. Brown ; 1859, Rev. J. B. Gould ; 1861, Rev. J. A. M. Chapman, the present pastor. The membership of the church in 1861 was 220, being an increase since 1851 of 120. Number of scholars connected with the Sabbath School, 270 ; average attendance, 225.

CHRIST'S CHURCH,

At Globe Village, was organized in 1849, and its house of worship dedicated in 1850. There were no pastors installed. Rev. S. S. Ashly, Rev. Mr. Harmon and Rev. Mr. Cummins, supplying the pulpit until 1854, when the church was disbanded, and their house purchased by the Rev. David Patten, for the use of the Methodist Episcopal Church.

THE METHODIST EPISCOPAL CHURCH

Was organized in the autumn of 1854. The names of pastors who have been connected with it since that time, are, Rev. A. H. Worthing ; Rev. C. A. Merrill ; Rev. A. U. Swinerton ; Rev. Elihu Grant, the present pastor. The membership of the church in 1861 was 34. Average attendance at the Sabbath School, 150.

THE CHURCH OF THE NEW JERUSALEM

Was organized in November, 1854, by the Rev. Thomas Worcester, of Boston. It then consisted of seven members. The present number is thirteen. It has no pastor, but its services are conducted by a leader, who is annually elected by the Society. It has ministerial services four times a year, usually, and sometimes oftener.

The average attendance at its meetings is between 30 and 40 persons. The average attendance at the Sabbath School is 26. The meetings are held in the room formerly occupied by the Young Men's Christian Association on Main street.

Mr. John Westall has been the leader and conductor of the services in this church, from its organization to the present time.

According to these statistics the total number of communicants connected with the various churches is 2,341, and the total number of pupils in Sabbath Schools, 2,918.

MISSION SCHOOLS.

In 1816 our town was a vineyard of the Massachusetts Home Missionary Society, into which she sent laborers, to toil and sow the seed of christian doctrine and teaching. The seed soon sprung up, and under the culture of the vine-dressers, the dews of the spirit, and the showers of grace, became a strong and spreading vine, shedding the sweet fragrance of christianity here and there, and gladdening the hearts of the laborers with large clusters of heavenly fruit.

Many churches were subsequently established here, strong in the faith of the Lord Jesus, which, in their turn, send forth men and money for the culture of other vineyards.

From time to time branches of domestic missionary effort have been shooting out from this vine. Perhaps the one most worthy of notice was that which appeared in the spring of 1853, called, "The Fall River Domestic Missionary Society." This Society had for its object "the diffusion of religious knowledge among the destitute in Fall River and vicinity, by the employment of one or more missionaries to labor from house to house, and by the distribution of Bibles, Tracts, and religious books." It chose for its missionary Mr. Thomas

Boardman, who labored under its patronage with devotion and acceptance, about four years and a half.

This effort in the form of a Society continued five years. Richard Borden, Benjamin Earl, Elihu Grant, and Jeremiah Young,
acted successively as Presidents.

A Ladies' Society was formed, auxiliary to this, in the summer of
1853, for the purpose of supplying clothing for Sabbath School children. It continued in existence nearly six years, and gave out hun-
dreds of garments to destitute children. Under the auspices of these
societies, and the labors of the missionary, three Sabbath Schools
were sustained. One which had been commenced in the summer of
1851, by two or three ladies in a private room, and afterwards transferred to the vestry of the Central Church, was organized as a Union
School. Two others were commenced—one in the south-west part
of the town, and one at New Boston. These schools continued their
operations after the societies were dissolved.

In connection with the first mentioned school a Sabbath School
Society was organized May 28th, 1854, called, "The Fall River Mission Sabbath School Society," which controls its affairs. At a meeting held May 28, 1860, a committee was appointed to relieve the
school from embarrassment in regard to a place for holding its ses-
sions, and authorized to provide a place free of expense to the Society.

Through the benevolent assistance of the friends of the school,
they offered to the Society the use of the chapel on Pleasant street,
which they entered February, 1861.

In June, 1859, the First Baptist Church assumed the care of the
school in the south-west part of the city, and a chapel was built on
Spring street, for its use, which they entered in June, 1861. At
the present time, 1862, there are connected with the several schools
as follows :

Fall River Mission Sabbath School, Pleasant street Chapel ;
                    Superintendents and teachers, 41 ; scholars, 438.
First Baptist Mission Sabbath School, Spring street Chapel ;
                    Superintendents and teachers, 22 ; scholars, 167.
New Boston Mission Sabbath School ;
                    Superintendents and teachers, 12 ; scholars, 90.
Three other Mission Schools sustained in suburbs of the city ;
                    Superintendents and teachers, 20 ; scholars, 150.
        Total—Superintendents and teachers, 95 ; scholars 845.

MANUFACTORIES. — COTTON MILLS.

The following statistics show, as nearly as can be obtained, the present extent of the cotton business in this city:

NAME OF MILL.	Date of Incorporation of Company.	No. of Spindles.	No. of Looms.	Bales Cotton used per annum.	Yards of Cloth manufactured.	No. of persons employed.	Quality of Cloth manufactured.	Power Used.	Capital of Company.
Troy Cotton and Woolen Manufac'ng Company,	1814	38,786	888	4,000	9,500,000	430	Print Cloths	Steam&Water.	$300,000
Fall River Manufactory,	1820	9,240	209	725	2,000,000	143	do.	Water.	150,000
Pocasset*	1822	18,048	374	3,000	3,500,000	297	39in.Sheet's	"	800,000
Quequechan		16,200	490	1,600	4,000,000	260	Print Cloths	"	
Anawan	1825	7,704	193	625	1,675,000	135	do.	"	160,000
Metacomet†		23,808	600	2,300	6,250,000	312	do.	Steam&Water.	
Massasoit Steam Mill,	1846	14,448	356	1,560	3,300,000	225	do.	Steam.	120,000
Watuppa Manufac'ng Company,	1848	11,000	300	1,000	2,000,000	180	do.	Water.	75,000
American Linen Mill,‡		31,500	700	3,000	7,400,000	350	do.	Steam.	400,000
Union Mill	1859	15,456	368	1,675	4,000,500	182	do.	Steam.	175,000
Robeson's Mill,§	1859	6,480	168	650	1,600,000	100	do.	Water.	80,000
Total,		192,620	4,576	20,135	45,225,500	2614			$2,260,000

*The Pocasset and Quequechan Mills belong to the Pocasset Manufacturing Company, which was incorporated in 1822. The Quequechan Mill now manufactures, on a part of its loops, 33 inch shirtings. Formerly only print cloths were produced, and of these, 4,000,000 yards were manufactured per annum.

†The Metacomet Mill is owned by the Fall River Iron Works Company, and was built by it in 1846.

‡See page 87.

§This Mill belongs to the Fall River Print Works Company, and since 1858, when the manufacture of cotton was substituted for printing, it has been generally called, Robeson's Mill.

In 1812 there were in Massachusetts but twenty cotton mills, with 17,371 spindles. In 1813 the first mill built in Fall River (see page 31) commenced operations with 896 spindles.

In 1840 there were eight mills, with 32,084 spindles, and 1,042 looms, (page 32).

THE AMERICAN LINEN COMPANY.

The American Linen Company was established in 1852, with a capital of $350,000, for the purpose of manufacturing, on a large scale, the finer linen fabrics. They erected buildings of stone—a factory 300 feet by 63, four stories high, with store and heckling house 150 feet by 48 ; a bleach house 176 feet by 75, and a finishing building 176 feet by 45, three stories high, with 10,500 spindles and 300 looms.

In the spring of 1853, they sent their first productions into the market. These consisted of blay linens, coating and pantaloon linen, sheetings, pillow and table linen, hucabuc and damask toweling, crash and diaper, which were highly approved by the trade. But before the mill was in full operation, the demand for such goods as the Company proposed to manufacture almost entirely ceased, for the reason that cotton and thin woolen fabrics were very generally substituted for linen goods. On this account it was determined, in the year 1858, to remove the machinery from the main mill into the outer buildings, and substitute machinery for the manufacture of cotton printing cloths. Another story was added to the mill, and 31,500 spindles, and 700 looms were set up.

The Company still retain, of their linen machinery, 3,500 spindles and 150 looms, which consume 400 tons of flax per year, and produce 1,500,000 yards of hucabuc, toweling, crash and diaper, and give employment to 200 operatives.

THREAD MILLS.

A Thread Mill was established in 1838, by Oliver Chace. It was sold to the present proprietor, Benjamin A. Chace, in January, 1862. The capital employed is $125,000. Number of operatives in the mill, 200. Number of spindles, 7,000. Nine hundred pounds of cotton are used, and 800 pounds of thread manufactured per day. The works are driven by one water wheel and two steam engines.

J. M. Davis' Thread Mill is situated in what was formerly Fall River, R. I. In this mill the thread is spooled, but not manufactured.

WAMSUTTA STEAM WOOLEN MILL.

Began the manufacture of woolen goods in 1849. The mill contains six cards, with thirty-six looms, manufacturing 150,000 yards of fancy cassimeres per annum, from 150,000 lbs. of wool. The number of persons employed is about 100. The machinery is driven by an engine of sixty horse power.

———

I. Buffinton & Son are owners of a Cotton Batt Manufactory, at Sucker Brook. They use about 1,500 bales of cotton per year.

———

Augustus Chace is proprietor of a Yarn, Wicking and Batt Manufactory at Mount Hope Village.

PRINT WORKS.

———

THE AMERICAN PRINT WORKS

Was established in 1834. The number of yards printed per annum is 15,000,000. Number of persons employed is 275. The works are driven by water power and three steam engines of about 350 horse power.

THE BAY STATE PRINT WORKS

Are now leased to the American Print Works Co. They print 11,000,000 yards of cloth per annum, and employ 200 persons. Motive power, one steam engine.

FALL RIVER IRON WORKS.

The Fall River Iron Works Company was incorporated in 1825, with a capital of $200,000, which capital, in 1845, was increased to its present amount, $1,000,000. The works are carried on in three buildings—a Rolling Mill, Nail Mill, and Foundry.

The Rolling Mill is 412 feet in length and 100 in breadth. The Nail Mill is 226 feet in length and 44 in breadth.

The machinery in the Rolling Mill is driven by one water wheel and three steam engines; in the Nail Mill by one steam engine. The number of puddling and heating furnaces is 24. Number of tons of coal consumed per annum, 12,000. Amount of pig iron worked, 6,000 tons; of scrap, 4,000; of bloom and billet, 300. Number of tons of castings produced, 1,500; of hoop and bar iron rods, &c., 3,000.

There are 106 nail machines, which manufacture 112,000 kegs of nails per annum. When in full operation, the mills require 600 workmen.

THE FALL RIVER GAS COMPANY

Commenced operations in 1847. The works are owned by the Fall River Iron Works Co., and consume about 1,000 tons of coal per annum.

FLOUR MILLS.

THE MASSASOIT FLOUR MILLS

Use eight runs of stone—six for flour and two for feed; manufacture 200 bbls. of flour daily, and employ about twenty hands. They turn out several qualities of flour, the brand of the best being Massasoit. The machinery is driven by an engine of 250 horse power. The mills were established in 1852, and are owned by Messrs. S. A. Chace and E. C. Nason.

M

THE BRISTOL COUNTY FLOUR MILLS

Were established in 1852. They use 4 runs of stone, manufacture 80 barrels flour daily, and employ 12 hands. Bristol County is the brand of their best grade of flour. The motive power is an engine of 120 horse power. D. A. Brayton proprietor.

THE FALL RIVER FLOUR MILLS

Were established in 1861; use 3 runs of stone; manufacture 25 barrels flour and 300 bags meal daily, and employ 5 hands. Brand of flour, Fall River Mill. Motive power, one engine of 40 horse power. D. Brown & Son proprietors.

MISCELLANEOUS STATISTICS.

BANKS.

THE FALL RIVER UNION BANK

Was incorporated in 1823, with a nominal capital of $200,000—the same amount as at the present time. The President is Nath'l B. Borden, elected in 1845. The President preceding him was David Durfee. The Cashier is D. A. Chapin, elected in 1860, the successor of Wm. Coggeshall.

THE FALL RIVER BANK

Was incorporated in 1825, with a capital of $100,000. The present capital is $350,000. David Anthony has been President of the Bank since its establishment, and H. H. Fish, Cashier since 1836.

THE FALL RIVER INSTITUTION FOR SAVINGS

Was incorporated in 1828. In 1856 the name was changed to *Fall River Savings Bank*. The President from 1828 to 1857, was Micah H. Ruggles; from 1857 to the present time, Nathaniel B.

Borden. Treasurer since 1836, J. F. Lindsey. The number of depositors, according to the last annual report, was 5,710. The amount on deposite, $1,759,745.

THE MASSASOIT BANK

Was incorporated in 1846, with a capital of $100,000. The present capital is $200,000. Jason II. Archer was President from 1846 to 1852. Israel Buffinton from 1852 to the present time. Cashier since 1846, Leander Borden.

THE SAVINGS BANK

Was incorporated in October, 1851. In that year Joseph Osborn was chosen President, and Wm. H. Brackett Treasurer, and they have held those offices to the present date. Number of depositors in February, 1862, was 1,439. Amount on deposite, $694,767.

THE METACOMET BANK

Was incorporated in 1853, with a capital of $400,000, which is now increased to $600,000. The Bank organized with Jefferson Borden, President, and A. S. Tripp, Cashier, which gentlemen have been continued in office to the present time.

THE POCASSET BANK

Was incorporated in May, 1854, with a capital of $200,000, the same amount as at the present date. Oliver Chace was President from June, 1854, to January, 1862, when Samuel Hathaway was elected to that office. Wm. H. Brackett has held the office of Cashier from June, 1854, to the present time.

THE FALL RIVER FIVE CENTS SAVINGS BANK

Was incorporated January, 1856, with the same President and Treasurer as now hold office, S. A. Chace and C. J. Holmes. The number of depositors is 2,450. Amount on deposite, $160,000.

THE WAMSUTTA BANK

Was incorporated in October, 1856, with the same capital as at the present time, $100,000. S. A. Chace has held the office of President, and C. J. Holmes that of Cashier, since the organization of the Bank.

OLD COLONY AND FALL RIVER

RAIL ROAD COMPANY.

On the 21st of March, 1844, a charter was obtained for building a rail road from Fall River to Myricks, and in June of the following year the first passenger train was run over the completed Fall River railway. In December, 1846, the route was opened as far as South Braintree, there connecting with the Old Colony road to Boston.

Through travel from Boston to New York by way of Fall River, commenced in May, 1847. In 1854, the two corporations—the Old Colony and the Fall River rail roads—were united under the name of the Old Colony and Fall River Rail Road Company. Their capital was then, and is at the present time, $3,015,100.

In 1861, a charter was obtained for extending the Old Colony and Fall River Rail Road through the city to the Rhode Island line. A charter was previously obtained from the Rhode Island Genral Assembly, to construct a road from Newport to this point. The road from Fall River to Newport is in process of construction at the present time.

THE BAY STATE STEAMBOAT COMPANY

Was incorporated in 1849, with a capital of $300,000. Richard Borden has held the office of President, and James S. Warner, the offices of Clerk and Treasurer, since the organization of the Company. The first boats that connected with the Fall River Rail Road, on the route between Boston and New York, were the Massachusetts and Bay State. These began running in May, 1847. The Empire State was placed on the route in June, 1848, and the Metropolis in 1855. The Company now own the Metropolis, of 2,108 tons, length of deck 340 feet; the Empire State, of 1,598 tons, length of deck 320 feet; the Bay State, of 1,554 tons, length of deck 320 feet; and the State of Maine, of 800 tons, length of deck 237 feet.

CUSTOM HOUSE.

The following statistics, compared with those given on page 34, will show the variation in the commerce of this place since 1840.

The number of vessels owned in the District of Fall River in 1850, was 85 ; in 1860, 123.

Tonnage of the District in 1850, 11,312 tons ; in 1860, 14,204 tons.

In 1850, the number of vessels employed in the whale fishery was 3, with a total tonnage of 865 tons ; in 1860, 2 vessels ; tonnage, 493.

Number of seamen employed in the District in 1850, was 500 ; in 1860, 518.

Number of foreign entries in 1850, was 39 ; in 1860, 15.

American tonnage entered from foreign countries in 1850, 3,179 ; in 1860, 1,446.

Amount of coal imported in 1850, 7,844 tons ; in 1860, 2,771.

No iron has been imported since 1850.

Amount of duties collected in 1850, $5,435 ; in 1860, $1,928.

In 1850, there were owned in the port of Fall River, 40 vessels, with a total tonnage of 8,816 tons ; in 1860, 61 vessels, with a tonnage of 14,204 tons.

POPULATION AND VALUATION

OF FALL RIVER.

YEAR.	POPULATION.	VALUATION, REAL AND PERSONAL.
1840	6,738	$2,989,468
1845	10,290	5,698,740
1850	11,170	7,423,665
1855	12,740	9,768,420
1860	13,240	11,522,650
1862	17,262	

Increase of population obtained in March, 1862, by change of Massachusetts and Rhode Island Boundary, 3,593.

NUMBER OF DEATHS AND BIRTHS
IN EACH YEAR SUBSEQUENT TO 1845.

YEARS.	DEATHS	BIRTHS	YEARS.	DEATHS	BIRTHS	YEARS.	DEATHS	BIRTHS
1846	209	382	1851	179	317	1856	401	497
1847	186	403	1852	220	411	1857	436	504
1848	218	364	1853	381	420	1858	301	507
1849	167	342	1854*	451	315	1859	329	517
1850	176	309	1855	326	322	1860	373	505
						1861	468	532

*The cholera made its appearance in this city on the 24th of August, 1854, and continued its ravages until October 5th, of the same year—a period of six weeks,—during which time one hundred and nineteen persons died of the disease.

PUBLIC SCHOOLS.

DATE.	No. of Schools.	Census of Children in School Districts.*	Am'nt Expended by the Town.	State Appropriation.	DATE.	No. of Schools.	Census of Children in School Districts.	Am'nt Expended by the Town.	State Appropriation.
1843	19	1943	$5213	$255	1853	25	2658	$11724	$551
1844	24	2135	4762	270	1854	26	2761	12979	625
1845	21	2372	5538	309	1855	27	2718	13479	602
1846	22	2727	6119	392	1856	31	2738	14905	603
1847	21	2611	6900	421	1857	31	2880	14467	556
1848	21	2786	9140	455	1858	30	2833	16084	612
1849	26	2834	9629	448	1859	31	2781	16038	594
1850†	26	2502	10179	453	1860	31	2855	17122	584
1851	26	2510	10930		1861	32	3221	17552	585
1852	27	2477	11403	539					

*On and after 1850, the Committee numbered only those between the ages of five and fifteen; previously they included all between four and sixteen.

†In this year the High School was established. George B. Stone was its Principal until May, 1855; from that time until August, 1858, James B. Pearson; and since 1858, Charles B. Goff.

CITY LIBRARY.

In 1860, arrangements were made by the City Government for the establishment of a free circulating library, and an appropriation was made for that object, and a room prepared in the City Building for the reception of books. According to agreement, the library of the Fall River Athenæum (pp. 38) was transferred to this room, and placed, with certain restrictions, at the disposal of the government. The books thus contributed were valued at $3,000.

The library was opened for circulation May 1, 1861. From the Librarian's report of January 13, 1862, it appears that there were received from the Athenæum, 2,362 volumes; by donation, 229; by purchase, 541; total, 3,132.† Number of magazines and papers received, 15. Average number of books circulated per day, 90. Number of volumes delivered from May 1, 1861, to May 1, 1862, 30,252.

The officers of the library are :—*Trustees*, E. P. Buffinton, Henry Lyon, Walter Paine, 3d, P. W. Leland, Simeon Borden, Samuel M. Brown, and C. J. Holmes. *Librarian*, George A. Ballard.

NEWSPAPERS AND PERIODICALS.

TITLE OF PAPER.	Established.	ISSUED.	Discontin'd.	Editors or Publishers.
Fall River Monitor, . . .	1825	Weekly.	1861	{ Nathan Hall to 1829, Benj. Earl to 1836, Henry Pratt to 1861.
Moral Envoy, ...	1830	"	1831	George W. Allen.
Weekly Recorder, . . .	1832	"	1836	Noel A. Tripp.
Fall River Patriot, . . .	1837	"	1840	William Canfield.
Archetype, ...	1841	"	1842	Louis Lapham & Thos. Almy.
Fall River Gazette, . . .	1842	"	1842	Abraham Bowen.
The Argus, ...	1842	"	1843	Jonathan Slade & Thos. Almy.
The Wampanoag, . . .	1842	Semi-Mo.	1842	Frances Harriet Whipple.
All Sorts, ...	1841	Weekly.	1860	Abraham Bowen.
The Mechanic, ...	1844	"	1845	Thomas Almy.
Weekly News, ...	1845	"	*	Thos. Almy & John C. Milne.
Mass. Musical Journal, . .	1855	Semi-Mo.	1856	E. Tourjee.
The Key Note, ...	1855	"	1856	"
Evening Star, . . .	1857	Daily.	1858	Noel A. Tripp & B. W. Pierce.
The Beacon, ...	1858	"	1859	Noal A. Tripp.
The Daily News, ...	1859	"	*	Thos. Almy and John C. Milne.
The People's Press, . . .	1859	Semi-W'ly	*	Noel A. Tripp.

Those marked thus * are still continued.

SHOPS, STORES, &c.

The number of shops and stores in Fall River in 1861, was about 400. There were 5 Apothecaries, 22 Boot and Shoe dealers and makers, 6 Printers, 4 Carriage builders, 18 Dry Goods merchants, 64 Grocers, 13 Physicians, and 6 Watch makers and Jewelers.

†Since this report was published, 240 volumes have been added to the Library—making the total, at the present time, 4,372.

LIST OF PERSONS

WHO HAVE FILLED THE SEVERAL TOWN OFFICES NAMED

SINCE 1840.

Town Clerk.—Benjamin Earl from 1836 to 1846. George Baker from 1846 to 1848. Samuel B. Hussey from 1848 to 1852. John R. Hodges in 1852 and 1853.

SELECTMEN.

1840—Nathaniel B. Borden, Israel Anthony, William Read.
1841—Matthew C. Durfee, Israel Anthony, William Read.
1842—Jervis Shove, Stephen K. Crary, George Brightman.
1843—Jervis Shove, Israel Anthony, Perez Mason.
1844—Thomas D. Chaloner, Israel Anthony, Perez Mason.
1845—Thomas D. Chaloner, Israel Anthony, Perez Mason.
1846—Israel Anthony, Leander Borden, James M. Morton.
1847—Azariah Shove, Israel Anthony, Benjamin Earl.
1848—Benjamin Wardwell, Israel Anthony, Benjamin Earl.
1849—Thomas J. Pickering, David Perkins, Benjamin Earl.
1850—David Perkins, Thomas J. Pickering, Daniel Brown.
1851—Thomas J. Pickering, James Buffinton, Daniel Brown.
1852—James Buffinton, Chester W. Greene, Geo. O. Fairbanks, Azariah Shove, Leander Borden.
1853—James Buffinton, Chester W. Greene, Thomas T. Potter, George O. Fairbanks, Azariah Shove.

GENERAL SCHOOL COMMITTEE.

1840—Orin Fowler, Asa Bronson, James Ford, Eliab Williams, Joseph Lindsey, Jonathan S. Thompson, George M. Randall.
1841—Joseph Lindsey, William H. A. Crary, George M. Randall.
1842—George M. Randall, William H. A. Crary, John Westall.
1843—George M. Randall, William H. A. Crary, John Westall.
1844—Henry Willard, Joseph F. Lindsey, Jonathan Slade, Louis Lapham, John Gregory.
1845—William H. A. Crary, David Perkins, Samuel B. Hussey.
1846—William H. A. Crary, Charles Aldrich, Samuel Washburn.
1847—William H. A. Crary, David Perkins, Charles Aldrich.
1848—Charles Aldrich, George O. Fairbanks, P. W. Hathaway.
1849—George O. Fairbanks, Henry Willard, Samuel Longfellow.

1850—George O. Fairbanks, Samuel Longfellow, Henry Willard, Eli Thurston, Jason H. Archer, Thomas Wilbur, Jesse Eddy.

1851—Samuel Longfellow, Jesse Eddy, Eli Thurston, Emery M. Porter, Azariah S. Tripp, Robert T. Davis.

1852—Azariah S. Tripp, Eli Thurston, James M. Aldrich, David A. Wallace, Jerome Dwelly.

1853—David A. Wallace, Eli Thurston, James M. Aldrich, Azariah S. Tripp, Jerome Dwelly, Job G. Lawton, Benjamin H. Davis.

1854—Eli Thurston, James M. Aldrich, Azariah S. Tripp, Jerome Dwelly, Benjamin H. Davis, Job G. Lawton.

CITY GOVERNMENT.

In the month of January, 1854, the inhabitants of the town of Fall River appointed a committee, consisting of nine individuals, to draft a City Charter. This committee prepared and presented a Charter, which was accepted, with some amendments, at a meeting of the towns-people, on the eighteenth of February ; 124 voting for and 51 against it. The same committee was authorized to apply to the Legislature for an act of incorporation for a City Government.

The Charter, as accepted by the town, was passed by the Legislature. April 11, 1854, the Senate voted it to be engrossed. April 12, the governor affixed his signature, and it became a law, making Fall River the thirteenth City incorported by the State of Massachusetts.

April 23, in town meeting, the Charter was accepted, 529 votes being cast for and 247 against it.

This Charter provided for the annual election on the first Monday in March, of City Officers ; consisting of a Mayor, and one Alderman and three Common Councilmen from each of the six wards into which the city was to be divided ; this Government to be organized on the first Monday in April. But by an amendment of the Charter in 1860, the time of election and organization was changed to December and January, three months earlier.

Since the incorporation of the City, the following persons have been elected to fill its several offices :

CITY CLERK.

John R. Hodges, from 1854 to 1855, and Alvin S. Ballard, from 1855 to the present time.

MAYOR.

James Buffinton, from 1854 to November, 1855, when he resigned, and was succeeded by Edward P. Buffinton, who continued in office until 1857. Nathaniel B. Borden, in 1857 ; Josiah C. Blaisdell, from 1858 to 1860 ; and Edward P. Buffinton, from 1860 to the present time.

ALDERMEN.

1854—James Henry, Edward P. Buffinton, Oliver Hathaway, Alvan S. Ballard, Edwin Shaw, Julius B. Champney.

1855—James Henry, Edward P. Buffinton, resigned Nov. 12, William M. Cook, elected Nov. 24, Oliver H. Hathaway, Isaac L. Hart, Edwin Shaw, Major Borden.

1856—James Henry, William M. Cook, James M. Osborn, John P. Slade, James Ford, David A. Brayton, resigned Oct. 13, Smith Winslow, elected Nov. 4.

1857—James Henry, South'd H. Miller, resigned Jan. 18, Joshua Remington, elected Jan. 27, John P. Slade, William Mason, 2d, William Carr.

1858—William Hill, Joshua Remington, James M. Osborn, Walter C. Durfee, Charles O. Shove, Ellis Gifford.

1859—James Henry, Nathaniel B. Borden, Ebenezer Luther, Walter C. Durfee, Charles O. Shove, Benjamin Earl.

1860—James Henry, Nathaniel B. Borden, Asa Pettey, Jr., John P. Slade, Charles O. Shove, William B. Durfee.

1861—Geo. H. Eddy, Nathaniel B. Borden Asa Pettey, Jr., John Mason Jr., James Ford, Job B. Ashly.

1862—Joseph Borden, Nathaniel B. Borden, Asa Pettey, Jr., John Mason, Jr., James Ford, Job B. Ashley.

GENERAL SCHOOL COMMITTEE.

1855—Eli Thurston, Azariah S. Tripp, Jerome Dwelly, Benjamin H. Davis, James M. Aldrich, Joseph E. Dawley, S. Angier Chace.

1856—James Ford, Azariah S. Tripp, James M. Aldrich, Jerome Dwelly, Joseph E. Dawley, Ebenezer T. Larned, S. Angier Chace.

1857—S. Angier Chace, Azariah S. Tripp, James M. Aldrich, Almadus W. Tripp, Emery M. Porter, James W. Hartley, Robert E. Barnett.

1858—Azariah S. Tripp, William Maclaren, James M. Aldrich, Robert E. Barnett, James W. Hartley, Almadus W. Tripp, Emery M. Porter.

1859—William Maclaren, Eli Thurston, Azariah S. Tripp, Emery M. Porter, Almadus W. Tripp, Warren Hathaway, S. Angier Chace.

1860—William Maclaren, Azariah S. Tripp, Seth Pooler, Joseph E. Dawley, Jerome Dwelly, J. Lewis Diman, James M. Aldrich.

1861—William Maclaren, Azariah S. Tripp, Joseph E. Dawley, Foster Hooper, Charles A. Snow, Simeon Borden.

1862—William Maclaren, Azariah S. Tripp, Joseph E. Dawley, Foster Hooper, Charles A. Snow, Simeon Borden.

MEMBERS OF CONGRESS

FROM FALL RIVER.

Nathaniel B. Borden, Orin Fowler, and James Buffinton, have been Representatives to the Congress of the United States, subsequent to 1840.

NAMES OF SENATORS AND REPRESENTATIVES

TO THE MASSACHUSETTS LEGISLATURE.

SENATORS.

Foster Hooper, 1840-42: P. W. Leland, 1843; N. B. Borden, 1845-47; Orin Fowler, 1848; Richard Borden, 1854: Joseph E. Dawley, 1855-56; Jeremiah S. Young, 1857; Robert T. Davis, 1859-61.

REPRESENTATIVES.

1842—Jonathan Slade, King Dean, William H. Ashley.
1843—Jonathan Slade, Wm. A. Waite, Wm. V. Read.
1844—Simeon Borden, Sen., Thomas D. Chaloner, Nathan Durfee.
1845—Simeon Borden, James B. Luther, Benjamin F. White.
1846—Chas. J. Holmes, Benj. W. Miller, Albert G. Eaton.
1847—David Perkins, Benj. Earl, Benj. W. Miller.
1848—David Perkins, Hezekiah Battelle, Wm. R. Robeson.
1849—Simeon Borden, Benj. Wardwell, James Ford, 2d.
1850—Iram Smith, Azariah Shove.
1851—Nath'l B. Borden, Richard Borden, J. B. Luther, Richard C. French.
1852—Nathan D. Dean, Iram Smith, E. P. Buffinton, Southard H. Miller.
1853—None.
1854—Mark A. Slocum, Job G. Lawton.
1855—Daniel Leonard, Asa P. French, Jona. E. Morrill, Benj. H. Davis.
1856—Brayton Slade, Jona. E. Morrill, John S. Brayton, Job B. Ashley.
1857—Jona. E. Morrill, Vernon Cook, Brownell W. Woodman, John E. Grouard.
1858—Josiah C. Blaisdell, Jonathan E. Morrill.
1859—Stephen C. Wrightington, Thomas T. Potter.
1860—Lloyd S. Earl, Stephen C. Wrightington.
1861—Lloyd S. Earl, Stephen C. Wrightington.
1862—Simeon Borden, Henry Pratt.

www.ingramcontent.com/pod-product-compliance
Lightning Source LLC
Chambersburg PA
CBHW022342020726
47500CB00004B/1237